Frank
and the
Flames
of Truth

Livi Michael has two sons, Paul and Ben, a
dog called Jenny and a hamster called Frank.
She has written books for adults before, but
ever since getting to know Frank has had the
sense that he had a story that should be told.
So here it is, and both Livi and Frank hope
you enjoy it very much.

LIVI MICHAEL

Frank and the Flames of Truth

Illustrated by Derek Brazell

PUFFIN BOOKS

*To the friends of Frank — who are now
too numerous to mention.*

*With special thanks to Ian Hunton, as ever, for
helping me to negotiate the tricky
underworld of electricity.*

PUFFIN BOOKS

Published by the Penguin Group
Penguin Books Ltd, 80 Strand, London WC2R 0RL, England
Penguin Group (USA) Inc., 375 Hudson Street, New York, New York 10014, USA
Penguin Books Australia Ltd, 250 Camberwell Road, Camberwell, Victoria 3124, Australia
Penguin Books Canada Ltd, 10 Alcorn Avenue, Toronto, Ontario, Canada M4V 3B2
Penguin Books India (P) Ltd, 11 Community Centre, Panchsheel Park,
New Delhi – 110 017, India
Penguin Group (NZ), cnr Airborne and Rosedale Roads, Albany, Auckland 1310, New Zealand
Penguin Books (South Africa) (Pty) Ltd, 24 Sturdee Avenue, Rosebank 2196, South Africa

Penguin Books Ltd, Registered Offices: 80 Strand, London WC2R 0RL, England

www.penguin.com

First published 2004
2

Text copyright © Livi Michael, 2004
Illustrations copyright © Derek Brazell, 2004
All rights reserved

The moral right of the author and illustrator has been asserted

Set in 13/15pt Bembo

Made and printed in England by Clays Ltd, St Ives plc

British Library Cataloguing in Publication Data
A CIP catalogue record for this book is available from the British Library

ISBN 0–141–31699–3

Contents

FRANK'S HOUSE
Guy lives here
MABEL'S HOUSE
Tania and her Mum and Dad live here
BRIGHT ST.
13
11
9

The Hamsters of Bright Street

GEORGE'S HOUSE
Jackie, Jake and Josh live here

ELSIE'S HOUSE
Lucy, Tom and their Mum and Dad live here

7 5 3 1

The WILD

Foreword

This is a story about a hamster called Frank who lives at number 13, Bright Street. Bright Street is a short, sloping row of terraced houses, and Frank lives in a cage in the front room of the end one. Originally, however, he came from the vast deserts of Syria and, while most hamsters adapt easily to living in a cage, Frank still felt the call of his ancient homelands, and the urge to be free. His Owner, Guy, was very fond of Frank, and treated him well; yet still, despite Guy's best efforts, Frank was always getting out and running away. He liked to explore the Spaces Between the houses, and especially to go into The Wild, a small area of waste land on the other side of Bright Street.

While travelling from one house to another, Frank had met the other hamsters who lived in Bright Street: Mabel, who lived next door at number 11, and Elsie, who lived at number 3. A hamster called George used to live at number 5, but he had met a hamster called Daisy, and they had decided to live together forever in The Wild. His place in the front room of number 5 Bright Street had been taken by a hamster called Maurice, but he was neither particularly friendly nor adventurous.

George and Elsie were Mabel's cubs, though she had never been very nice to them, and in fact had once tried to eat George. Mabel hadn't been very nice to Frank either. She had told him that the Call he kept trying to follow was an evil one, coming from a mythical beast known as the Black Hamster of Narkiz, who would entrap Frank and Lure him to the Pits of Doom. But Frank had followed the Call anyway and had met the Black Hamster. He had shown Frank the ancient city of Narkiz, and asked him to help his people, though he had never explained how. Frank knew there was something special he had to do to save the ancient tribe of Hamster, and he knew that only he could find out what it was.

The other thing you need to know about Frank is that he has a motto. His motto is 'Courage!' and it is very important, for without it he would never be able to find out what exactly it is that he has to do.

1 The Call

A good deal of noise was coming from the first house in Bright Street. New neighbours were moving in. Of course, moving house is a noisy business, but the people who lived in the other houses in Bright Street hadn't expected it to be quite this noisy. Music blared from the van, furniture crashed and thudded, and the new people bellowed at one another above the noise.

'*Mind the lamp!*' screeched the woman.

'**GET THAT SKATEBOARD OUT OF THE WAY**!' shouted the man.

'*DAD*!' roared the boy. '*I CAN'T FIND MY HEADPHONES*!'

Inside the other houses, tables rattled and shook, and in number 3 a picture fell off the wall.

'I've never heard anything like it,' said Arthur in number 9. 'There's only three of them moving in, and it sounds like an army!'

The new couple were called Mr and Mrs Walker, and their son was called Sean. They introduced themselves to Jackie when she wandered out to see what was happening, and to ask whether they needed any help.

'NO TA, LOVE,' shouted Mrs Walker. 'WE'RE JUST GETTING SORTED. I'M CHERYL, BY THE WAY, AND THIS IS MY SON, SEAN.'

Sean scowled at Jackie. He had a close-shaven head and a chain that hung between his ear and his nose. He looked about eleven.

'I'm Jackie,' Jackie started to say, but she was interrupted by a tremendous clatter from above as a drum kit rolled down the stairs. This was followed by furious swearing from the top landing.

'THAT'LL BE ERIC,' Cheryl said. 'I'D BEST GO AND HELP.'

'Well, if you need a hand –' Jackie began nervously, but Cheryl had already gone and Sean was now scowling even more ferociously, so she left them to it.

'Well,' she thought as she re-entered her own house, 'it's a good job Les and Angie aren't in.'

Les and Angie lived at number 3, next door to the new neighbours, with their children, Lucy and Thomas, and Lucy's hamster, Elsie, who was very disturbed by the noise. Hamsters like to sleep in the daytime, and she had been woken up several times by crashes and bangs and yells. She kept running out of her bed chamber to see what was going on.

'Oh, what's happening?' she thought. 'Is it an earthquake? Or a volcano?'

Elsie knew about earthquakes and volcanoes from when Lucy told her about her homework. Now she wished very much that Lucy was there to explain to her what was going on. But Lucy wasn't there, and now it sounded as though it might be the end of the

world, or at least as though all the houses in Bright Street were being demolished. Lucy's bedroom walls shook and the shelf on which Elsie's cage was standing rattled so much that she thought it might fall off. Elsie ran round her cage frantically a few times then curled up tightly in her bed and stuffed some of her bedding into her ears.

The new neighbours weren't the only ones making a lot of noise. It was a few days before bonfire night and children from other streets were invading the waste ground known to the hamsters as The Wild, dragging planks of wood and branches and broken chairs into a big pile. There was even an old settee that someone had thrown out.

As half term approached, older children gathered at night and lit fireworks that roared and hissed and banged. Arthur had been out several times to tell them off. 'It's dangerous, that's what,' he said. 'Big lads and girls like you – you're old enough to know better. It's not bonfire night yet!'

But the big boys and girls only called him grandad and asked if they could use his clothes for their guy. One of them even threw a firework after him.

Arthur was outraged. 'I'm calling the police,' he said, but of course, by the time the police got there, they had all disappeared.

No animal likes fireworks of course, and, as well as the hamsters, the cats were very upset. Jackie's big white cat, Sergeant, retreated under the table in the living room and squatted there, glaring, like an evil, hairy pillow with fluorescent eyes. And at number 7 Mrs Timms was out at least twenty times a day, calling in all the stray cats and fussing when one of them went missing. The wildlife was affected, too. The little shrews and voles and fieldmice scurried anxiously in and out of their holes, pouncing on food and whisking it away again. Spiders and beetles skulked in crevices and, by moonlight, foxes and owls flitted silently across the Waste Land, disconcerted by the great heap that was taking shape. The owls circled above it, the foxes sniffed it curiously, but both decided that, whatever it was, they didn't like the look of it, and they rapidly disappeared.

Inside the first hamster burrow that had ever been made in The Wild, George and Daisy were having a conference.

'Well, something's going on,' Daisy said. 'And I don't like it, I don't like it at all.'

George agreed. He had just pulled one of his cubs down from the surface, moments before there was an awful explosion and the smell of scorched earth. Now all the hamster cubs were grounded, and they weren't happy. It was evening, the time when hamsters come out to play. Normally this was the time when they would run around The Wild, exploring, foraging and playing hide and seek. They felt trapped and miserable in their burrow.

'We want to play, we want to play!' they chanted.

'Will you listen to them,' said Daisy, exasperated. 'I can't put up with that all night!'

'They don't understand the danger,' George said, and he frowned, because he didn't understand it himself. This was some new threat, and George thought he had lived in The Wild long enough to understand all its perils, but he had never encountered anything like this before. He wondered if Frank knew what was going on.

'I tell you what,' he said. 'I think we should all dig deeper and stay underground for a while. How about if I get them all digging a new burrow? That should keep them busy for a while.'

Daisy beamed at George. 'You always know the right thing to do,' she said. 'You're the best dad in the world,' and she nuzzled him briefly. George blushed.

Meanwhile, in her luxurious cage, Mabel wasn't happy at all.

'Whatever's going on?' she said as a firework went

off with a whistle and a sizzle. 'What's happening?' She leapt violently as someone let off a banger, then ran behind her wheel. Of course, no one thought to explain to her what was going on, though she did hear Tania's mum telling her that she was not, under any circumstances, to play on the waste ground while those naughty boys were messing about with fireworks.

'*Fireworks?*' she thought. She didn't know what they were, but she didn't like the sound of them. And over the next day or so the noise got worse. Explosions, shrieks and whistles, sizzling and cracking noises, then more bangs.

Mabel grew more and more nervous, and she wasn't the nervous type. It was the time of year when hamsters like to sleep more, but she couldn't sleep. The dreadful explosions began late in the afternoon and continued far into the night. Mabel's routine was disturbed, and she liked her routine. She liked the comfort and luxury of her cage, which was very splendid, but she found that she was too disturbed to do her usual cleaning and sorting and cage-management, and though she moved her bed several times she couldn't escape the noise.

'Hooligans!' she thought, gazing distractedly towards the window. Bits of sawdust clung to her pelt, which was usually immaculate. Mabel was very proud of her snowy pelt, but now she was ruffled. Finally, after a series of particularly loud explosions, she decided that she couldn't stand it any more. When all went quiet, she packed her pouches.

Mabel had never voluntarily left her terrain before. She had no interest in the world outdoors, even less in The Wild, but she had decided that there was only one thing she could do. She was going to see Frank.

Mabel didn't know exactly what she expected Frank to do, she just knew that he had to do something. He was the hamster who liked adventures, and the one who got things done. She didn't particularly like Frank, nor did she believe what he said about the Black Hamster. She was inclined, if the truth were told, to think Frank mad, especially when he talked about hamsters breaking free from captivity and going to live in The Wild. Mabel could imagine nothing worse than leaving the luxury of her own domain and going to live in a wild and frightening place where she had to hunt for her own food. But Frank was the only hamster she could think of who would do something about a Threatening Situation, and she was getting desperate. So that night, after the other members of her household had gone to bed and all was quiet, Mabel cautiously lifted the lid of her cage and clambered out.

She remembered the opening in the skirting board that Frank used when he visited and she headed for that now, through the soft pink fronds of carpet that were rather messy and tangled in places (Tania's mum wasn't big on housework). She found the opening without much difficulty and squeezed herself through with rather more difficulty because she was plumper than Frank and her pouches were very full. But, after a bit of squirming and thrusting and kicking, she was finally through to the sooty darkness of the Spaces Between.

Mabel took a while to adjust to the instant gloom. She felt like a different hamster outside her own territory, unsure of herself and afraid. She didn't like the different scents, of plaster and brick dust, wooden joist and drain. She didn't like the feeling of standing on fragments of loose slate and tiny stones, over which her paws slithered, or the various small objects that had somehow got trapped in the Spaces Between – scraps of material, drawing pins and a tiny wheel. Frank found all this kind of thing exciting and it made him want to explore further, but Mabel was dreadfully put off by the dirt and dust and strange sounds that reverberate through the Spaces Between. When a cobweb brushed her face, she squeaked out loud.

She told herself to keep calm. She knew from what Frank had said that she had to follow the wooden beam by her side. This was called the Main Joist and it ran beneath all the houses. As long as she kept the main joist at her side, Mabel told herself, she would be fine. It would take her straight to Frank's front room.

Several times Mabel almost changed her mind. Small stones and pieces of chipped slate hurt her paws, and the brick dust made her sneeze. Hamsters are nocturnal, and are used to darkness, but this was not the usual darkness of night. It was the complete absence of light, and air. Terrible images filled Mabel's mind: of hamsters that had been Lured away from the safety of their own cages or burrows and never returned. Every hamster knew that away from their own territory there was Danger; wild things lurked in shadows, or in pools where the water had gone bad. Mabel didn't really believe in the Black Hamster of Narkiz, or she thought she didn't, yet somehow, in these strange, neglected, dusty spaces, it was an image of this terrible beast that rose and hovered in the back of her mind.

'You're just being silly,' she told herself unconvincingly, and the image of the Black Hamster, which was the image of Fear itself, grinned and licked its bloodied lips.

Imagine how unhappy she was, therefore, when a voice other than her own spoke in the darkness. 'Mabel,' it said, and Mabel started violently and reared, ready to strike. But she couldn't see anything and this made her tremble all over.

For all her faults, however, Mabel did not lack courage, and she was determined to go down fighting. 'Who is it?' she said. 'Come out and show yourself at once!'

2 The Challenge

Frank was having a very peculiar day. First there had been The Grand Cage-Cleaning, which Guy only got round to every few weeks, so Frank never got used to it. Guy had put him in a little plastic globe-thing and Frank had to run round the room in it for what seemed like hours, bumping into the furniture. Twice he got stuck, first wedged behind a chair, then between Guy's guitar and the wall, and Guy was so busy talking on the phone he didn't even notice.

'Yeah – it's about time we got the band together again,' he was saying. 'But we'll have to rehearse –' Then there was a long discussion about where they might rehearse and what time they could all make it, and what songs they all knew, while poor Frank kicked and pushed and scrabbled but couldn't dislodge the globe. It was a new globe too, since Guy had got tired of sticking the lid of the old one down with tape. Frank had chewed the lid of the old one and could almost always get it off and wriggle out, but this new lid seemed to be sealed and hamster-proof. Frank stopped scrabbling for a moment and began patiently to investigate it, to see if there was anywhere he might start to nibble.

You should know that during Frank's first adventure, when he had met the Black Hamster for the first time, he had discovered that he had a strange kind of power over Guy. If Guy was relaxed and not thinking too hard, Frank could actually tap into his thoughts and make him do things. He had used this power to make sure he was fed regularly, with proper food, and taken out of his cage so that he could explore, and to make sure that Guy didn't seal off any of Frank's special exits and entrances to the Spaces Between. But also, it has to be said, he had sometimes used it for no good reason at all, to make Guy do silly things, like eating a bowl of hamster food or barking madly at the door when someone knocked. But ever since his last adventure, when Frank had rescued several hamsters from a sinister character called Vince, he had tried not to use his power irresponsibly. At that time he had met the Black Hamster again, and since then Frank had known that he had to be worthy of the task that the Black Hamster wanted him to do – whatever that task was. And so now, as Guy's interminable conversation continued, Frank patiently nibbled first at one section of the lid, then at another.

Even when Guy finished his conversation he didn't notice Frank. He went straight into the kitchen to make himself a stack of cheese-and-chutney sandwiches, leaving the cage half cleaned. Then finally he picked up his guitar.

'There you are, Frank!' he said eventually, picking the globe up.

'At last!' thought Frank, giving Guy an old-fashioned look.

But Guy didn't take him out of the globe. He put it down again on the carpet and sat down with his guitar, and Frank had to run around in it again while Guy sang songs to him.

O Frank you
Know I have to thank you
Just for being you
Dooby doo, dooby doo, dooby doo di doo . . .

Usually when Guy sang to him like this, Frank would curl up in his bedroom and stuff bits of bedding into his ears to shut out the noise, but now he had to roll around the carpet listening to one song after another:

Frank, we'll always be together
Till the very end
Just you me and the weather
I'll always be your friend . . .

'Well, stop singing then,' Frank thought crossly as he bumped into the legs of the table one more time, but Guy didn't.

We'll run away forever
And raise a fam-i-ly . . .

Frank thought this had gone far enough. He stopped rolling about and took a deep breath, but just as he was about to command Guy to shut up and put him back in his cage, Guy stopped.

'Time to put you back,' he said, to Frank's relief, and he took the lid off the globe and carried Frank back to his cage, which was still only half cleaned, with only half the amount of wood shavings Frank was used to. Frank ran round his cage, sniffing suspiciously.

'Oi!' he said. 'Where's my food?' And Guy trotted off obediently to get him some, talking all the time about how he was going to re-form the band he'd had in college.

Guy was in a funny mood for the rest of that day, even more dreamy than usual, yet curiously energized. Half an hour after putting Frank back in his cage he started shifting furniture around.

'If I clear some space,' he muttered, 'we can rehearse in here,' and he dragged the settee backwards and moved the table into the corner of the room, and put the telly on it. Then he picked up Frank's cage and Frank slid from one side of it to the other.

'Now, where shall I put you?' Guy murmured, gazing round the room for a suitable place. He tried the coffee table, but there wasn't enough room now that the telly was on it, then the window sill, but Frank objected loudly. He didn't mind being able to see out of the window, but he didn't want the sun to burn in on him. And the gas fire was too warm, but eventually Guy put him down on top of the old meter cupboard.

'There you are, Frank,' he said. 'Perfect!'

'Fine,' Frank muttered, picking up scraps of bedding and food that had fallen out while he was being moved. There wasn't such a good view from this part of the room, and all he could really see was the settee, but after so much rolling around he just wanted to be left in peace. 'Now leave me alone, please.'

Guy did leave him alone. It was time for him to put on his uniform and guide the schoolchildren across the road. He had taken this job under protest at first but had discovered that he quite liked it – it got him out of the house and talking to people, as Jackie had said.

Once he'd gone, Frank prepared to settle down. But then he became aware of a curious noise that seemed to come from beneath his cage: a very low-pitched humming noise that he hadn't noticed before. It faded, then, just as he was settling, it started again. Then, when he decided to ignore it, the first of the explosions started on The Wild.

'What's going on?' he thought, and he wondered if George and Daisy were safe, and whether he should try to find them. He had thought about this before, but first of all he'd been recovering from his big adventure in the sewer, then all the terrible noises had started, and the bangs and shrieks and sizzles made him nervous and wary.

'Courage,' he muttered to himself, as a particularly loud series of explosions began, and he stood with his paws raised, undecided. Then, just as he started to get out of his cage, the front door flew open and Guy hurried in.

'The little monsters!' he panted, quite pink in the face with wrath. 'They're throwing mudballs!'

Guy looked in a sorry state. His shiny new coat and lollipop sign had been pelted with mud and his hat had been knocked off. It was the same gang of boys and girls who were throwing fireworks on The Wild.

'And that new kid at number one's in with them,' he said. 'Just wait till I see his parents!' He went upstairs to clean up.

The rest of the evening Guy was in and out, talking to Jackie, knocking on the front door of number 1 (but they were playing music so loudly that they didn't hear him) and having long conversations with Arthur and

Les about what could be done. In the end he went to the pub with Les, and Frank was left alone. He could hear the humming sound again, but was so tired he felt he needed a little nap before investigating further. He curled up in his bed, determined to ignore all further noise, but, just as he was about to fall asleep, he heard: 'Frank! Wake up! Wake up! Wake up!' and the bars of his cage rattled furiously.

Frank opened one eye blearily. An enormous white ball with staring eyes was pressed up against the bars of his cage.

'Wake up! Wake up! Help!' it said.

Frank opened his other eye. 'Mabel?' he said.

Mabel was very agitated, and all her white fur was standing on end.

'Let me in,' she spluttered. 'It's behind me – back there – in the dark – you must help!' And she rolled her eyes back theatrically as though she might faint.

'What *are* you going on about?' Frank said, climbing out of his bed.

'Oh please let me in,' Mabel begged. 'I've been Lured!'

'Lured?' Frank said, as Mabel rolled her eyes and muttered. 'Whatever do you mean?'

'Just let me *in*!'

'No!' said Frank. He had never got on particularly well with Mabel, and Syrian hamsters are not especially sociable.

But Mabel kept wringing her paws and muttering, 'It's too late, it's too late!' until, in the end, Frank got out of his cage and let Mabel get in. He told her to have a drink of water and calm down.

Once in a cage again, Mabel did seem to calm down. She sniffed around it, making comments like 'Only one floor?' and 'No wonder you want to get away so much with a cage like this.'

'A cage is a cage, Mabel,' Frank said firmly. 'Now, are you going to tell me what's going on, or are you going to go away and let me get some sleep?'

'Oh don't send me back!' Mabel moaned piteously. 'I couldn't face that terrible journey again! I'll –'

'Then get on with it!' Frank said, losing patience. 'What's happened?'

Mabel preened her ruffled pelt. 'Well,' she began, and she told him that she'd been coming to see him, making her own way heroically through the Darkness and Dangers of the Spaces Between, when she'd heard the Voice – that Voice which all hamsters dread to hear – the Voice of the Force that Lures. 'Mabel,' it had said. Mabel's eyes were huge and haunted as she told her

tale. 'Mabel,' the voice had said again, and Mabel yelped as something brushed up against her, then she went into her War Pose and issued a volley of alarming squeaks. 'Mabel,' the voice said once more, and Mabel stopped, mid-squeak, her teeth bared, ready to fight.

'Frank?' she said, then, 'Show yourself now!'

But already she had realized that it was not Frank she could smell. This was an older scent, wild and strange. Mabel peered into the darkness, then, through the gloom, she saw red eyes gleaming.

'I wasn't scared, of course,' she said to Frank. She was much more nonchalant now that she knew she was safe. 'Is this your food?'

Frank could hardly contain his excitement. 'What happened?' he said, whiskers twitching and his own pelt beginning to lift.

'Well . . .' said Mabel, then, 'Is this that packet stuff you get in the shops?'

Frank hopped up and down. 'Get on with it!' he said.

'Don't mind if I do,' said Mabel, and she plunged her nose into Frank's bowl.

Frank stared at her as she gromphed his food. 'Er – you can have some if you like,' he said, then watched, fascinated, as all his food disappeared into Mabel at record speed.

'Not bad,' Mabel said, finally surfacing. 'A bit tasteless though – we generally have salmon croquettes on Thursdays. Now then, where was I?'

Frank glared at her. He was in two minds whether or not to simply order her out of his cage and get back to sleep. He'd had experience of Mabel's stories before and knew that she wasn't entirely truthful. On the other hand, *something* had frightened her in the Spaces Between, and if it had been the Black Hamster then he definitely wanted to know.

'Take your time,' he said, with just a touch of sarcasm.

Mabel combed out her long and exceptionally fine whiskers.

'Well,' she said, 'I drew myself up to my full height, and said to the − *thing* − whatever it was, "Back off, ruffian, and kindly allow me through. I want nothing to do with scoundrels from The Wild." '

Mabel declaimed this theatrically, striking an impressive pose, but looking at Frank out of the corner of her eye, she could see that he wasn't impressed.

'*And* − ?' he said. Mabel dropped down again into her usual pose and sniffed round for more food.

'And nothing,' she said. 'Whatever it was, it could tell it had met its match in me, and it simply − disappeared.'

Many thoughts ran through Frank's mind, not all of them pleasant. He took a deep breath. 'All right, Mabel,' he said. 'Now − what really happened?'

A few moments later, after some searching questions from Frank and protestations from Mabel, Frank felt that he had a more accurate picture of what had occurred. Mabel had definitely smelled a strange scent in the Spaces Between, and something had called her name. She had thought she had seen eyes glaring at her in the darkness, and had bolted.

'I wasn't *scared*,' she said again. 'I just thought it was

best to be on the safe side.'

Frank didn't know what to think. Perhaps it was Mabel's overactive imagination – he knew how she hated being away from her own territory. On the other hand, it did sound as if it could have been the Black Hamster – but why ever would he bother with Mabel? She had told lies about him in the beginning, making him out to be some kind of Bogey Hamster, and really she didn't even believe in him. 'Maybe it wasn't the Black Hamster at all,' Frank thought.

'What do you think it was?' he said, but Mabel almost seemed to have lost interest.

'Oh, I don't know,' she said airily. 'A rat, possibly – even a snake.'

'A *snake?*' Frank said.

'Strange things lurk in the Spaces Between,' said Mabel.

Frank thought. 'But it knew your name,' he said.

But Mabel obviously didn't want to talk about it any more. 'Whatever it is, it's gone now,' she said. 'And I didn't come here to discuss strange lurking things.'

'Why did you come here?' Frank queried.

Outside, a rocket squealed into the air before erupting into many colours.

'*That's* why,' said Mabel. 'I want you to stop all the noise.'

'What?' said Frank.

'It's gone on long enough,' Mabel said fretfully. 'Night after night – every time I try to get to sleep – it's wearing me down, I tell you, it's fraying my nerves. It's –'

'All right, all right,' Frank said. 'But what do you expect me to do about it?'

Mabel blinked at him. 'Well, you know,' she said. 'That's what you do, isn't it? Take things on. Sort stuff out.'

Frank began to feel that this conversation had gone on long enough.

'No, it isn't what I do, Mabel,' he said. 'I don't have supernatural powers – or at least,' he added, 'I don't have that kind of power. I don't like the noise either, but I'm just putting up with it. It'll go away eventually.'

'I don't want it to go away *eventually*,' Mabel said, baring her teeth. 'I want it to go away *now*.'

Frank could see that they weren't getting anywhere. 'Look, Mabel,' he said. 'I can see that you've gone to a lot of trouble to come here, and I'm flattered. But I think you're overestimating what I can do. We all have to put up with things we don't like. Now I'm sorry if I can't be more help –'

'*Sorry!*' said Mabel in disgust. 'I risk my life coming all this way to ask for your help, and you're *sorry*? Well – if you're not going to do anything about it, then what use are you? What are you *for*?'

'Now hold on a minute –' said Frank, beginning to lose his temper, but then he stopped. 'Did you hear that?' he said.

'Of course I heard it,' said Mabel, referring to a particularly loud banger. 'It practically blew my eardrums out!'

But Frank was listening to another noise: the

low-pitched humming he'd heard before. 'There it is again!' he said.

'Yes, that's what I'm trying to *tell* you!' said Mabel, exasperated. 'It never lets up – there's another one.' She retreated fearfully behind Frank's wheel.

'No – not the fireworks,' Frank said. 'Another noise – like a kind of – well – *humming*.'

'I don't know what you're talking about,' Mabel said petulantly.

But Frank was running along the edge of the meter cupboard. 'Sssh!' he said. 'There it is again!'

Mabel's pelt lifted because her nerves were still on edge. 'Where? What?' she said.

'That noise – can't you hear it?'

'What noise?' said Mabel. 'What are you going on about?'

But Frank only said '*Ssssh!*' again, quite violently this time.

'I'm going,' said Mabel, offended. 'I've had enough. I might have known not to ask a mad hamster for help. First you start *seeing* things, now you're *hearing* things – what does your Owner put in your food?' And she turned and began to climb out of Frank's cage.

'*Wait!*' Frank hissed so sharply that Mabel jumped again and, in spite of herself, turned round. 'You must be able to hear it – not explosions – a kind of – well – *humming*.'

'*Humming!*' Mabel said with scorn, but then it seemed to her that she *could* hear something. She paused, listening, but it disappeared.

Frank poked his head towards the cupboard door. 'I

can hear you, whatever you are,' he called. 'Come out and show yourself!' Then he waited and listened, but nothing happened. 'It's gone again,' he sighed. 'But I thought I could smell hamsters down there.'

'Hamsters?' said Mabel, 'Humming hamsters? Oh well!' she said. 'Why am I surprised? First you go on about dancing hamsters, now it's the humming hamsters – next they'll be skateboarding, or learning to knit.'

Frank didn't respond to this. He was still listening, puzzled. 'I don't think the hamsters are humming,' he said.

Mabel snorted. 'Well, of course they're not!' she said. 'It's probably just the ringing in your ears from all the explosions. Which you've so kindly said you're not going to do anything about – even though I've come all this way. I really don't know why I bothered.' And she turned again and climbed out on to the meter cupboard. 'Well,' she said. 'I'm waiting.'

'What for?' said Frank.

'For you to come back with me, of course.'

Frank shook his head. 'Why?' he asked.

'Well, I can't go back on my own,' said Mabel as though this was obvious.

'I thought you said you weren't scared,' said Frank.

'I'm not –' said Mabel, then suddenly her chin trembled. 'Oh, Frank,' she cried. 'Don't make me go back there alone – I can't do it – I can't. *Anything* could be out there! If you won't come back with me I'll – I'll – I'll have to stay with you!'

Frank sighed. But Mabel was already climbing back

into his cage, and that was the last thing he wanted. Besides, he was secretly curious. Suppose it *had* been the Black Hamster, and he was still there, waiting for Frank. Frank hadn't seen him for months and he had so many questions to ask. And it was obvious that he wasn't going to get any rest in his own bed.

'All right, Mabel,' he said, and Mabel smiled. 'I'll come back with you. But only as far as your skirting board, mind – I'll show you how to get through, and then you're on your own.'

'Thank you, Frank,' Mabel said, almost humbly, and she climbed out of his cage at once and followed him down the cracks in the side of the meter cupboard and across the carpet, along the ledge that ran underneath the gas fire, to the gap beneath, where a hamster could drop down easily into the Spaces Between.

There in the space beneath the floor, Mabel became again a nervous hamster, but Frank felt a familiar surge of excitement and the call of older instincts beckoning him on. He wanted to sniff everything and explore different routes. But Mabel kept clutching him in alarm every time she heard something, and the Spaces Between were full of strange noises, clicks and hollow tappings. Once, when there was an unexpected thudding, she leapt at Frank and almost sat on him, so in the end he followed the quickest pathway, along the main joist to the chink in the brickwork that led to the crack in the skirting board. All the time he listened and sniffed, trying to detect anything unusual, but there was nothing, and he had to stifle a feeling of disappointment.

'Well, here we are,' he said at last. 'You're back now. This is it.'

'Oh, thank goodness,' Mabel said. 'Oh, that was horrid. I'm so glad to be back!'

She waddled right up to the chink in the brickwork, ready to squeeze her way through, then she paused and looked at Frank in a knowing, rather cunning way.

'What were you looking for, back there?' she asked. 'I saw you sniffing about and checking everything.'

'Nothing,' said Frank.

'Yes, you were,' said Mabel. 'You were looking for,' she lowered her voice, 'the Black Hamster, weren't you?'

Frank didn't say anything.

'You thought it might have been him before, didn't you?' Mabel went on, still with the same cunning expression.

'It could have been anyone, or anything,' Frank said. 'It could have been your overactive imagination.'

Mabel shook her head. 'But you don't think it was, do you, Frank?' she said smoothly. 'You think it might have been him. And you're wondering why he was calling me, not you.'

Frank didn't like the way this was going.

'I thought you didn't believe in him,' he said.

Now Mabel looked coy. 'Well, I never *used* to,' she said, looking at Frank out of the corner of her eye. 'But, well, I certainly heard *something* calling me by name. Who else could it be?' When Frank said nothing, she said, 'What's the matter, Frank, hasn't he been calling you recently?'

This was a bit too near the bone. Frank said gruffly, 'He'll contact me, when the time comes.'

'Of course,' said Mabel sweetly. 'That is, unless he's not interested any more. Maybe he's moved on.'

Frank felt a flare of temper. 'Moved on to you, you mean?' he said.

'Well, why not?' said Mabel. 'You can't be the only hamster he wants to call, now, can you? Perhaps he's tired of calling you.'

'He's not *tired*,' said Frank. 'He doesn't get *tired*. And if he did, he wouldn't call you.'

'Well, something did,' said Mabel, still looking sly. 'And he doesn't seem to have been interested in you recently.'

'He'll call me when there's something he wants me to do,' said Frank, though not very confidently.

'Perhaps you should call him,' Mabel said, looking beadily at Frank. 'Or perhaps,' she continued, 'perhaps he wouldn't come if you did.'

Frank stared at her. He knew she was goading him, yet also she was voicing his secret thoughts. Would the Black Hamster come if he called? Into his mind came the words the Black Hamster had spoken to him when they had last met. '*Help my people.*' Surely that meant he'd come back to show Frank how, and maybe he was just waiting for Frank to be ready. Perhaps now was a good time, especially if he had been here just a short while ago. And that would certainly show Mabel.

Mabel was still watching Frank. 'You could always try,' she said silkily.

Frank took a deep breath. Then he closed his eyes.

Mabel watched him eagerly, poised for flight in case anything did happen. In Frank's mind there was a jumble of thoughts and memories, images of the first time he had followed the Black Hamster into The Wild and seen the whirling hamsters of Syria; then of the time when he had ridden on the back of the Black Hamster and seen the ancient hamster city of Narkiz; and the time when he had scared off Vince, an evil man intent on flaying hamsters for their pelts. When Frank had needed him, he'd been there, and surely now, after all this time of waiting, Frank did need him to come again. He tried to relax and find a clear, silent space in his mind.

'Please, please come,' he thought over and over again, but whether it was because Mabel was still watching him, or because he hadn't tried hard enough to empty his mind, nothing happened. He opened his eyes again and Mabel was looking at him with a peculiar kind of triumph.

Frank's mouth was dry. 'I can't do it,' he said.

'No?' said Mabel. 'I thought not.'

'It's not the right time –' Frank began but Mabel cut him short.

'You can't do it,' she said, 'because he doesn't exist! I knew all along,' she crowed. 'It's just a story to frighten cubs with. The Black Hamster!' she said with scorn.

'Now just a minute –' Frank said.

'And all this time you've been stringing the others along, and trying to Lure them into The Wild, where they'll be hunted and eaten! Instead of leaving them where every sensible hamster belongs – in a cage! Well,

I saw through you right from the start – there is no Black Hamster and I think we've just seen the proof of that – don't you?'

Furious, Frank reared. He would have lunged forward to bite Mabel but she scuttled backwards through the brick and plaster work, and the chink in the skirting board, until she was back in her own domain. Frank could hear her laughing at him on the other side of the skirting board, and for a moment he felt inclined to follow her and fight, but what was the use? Hamsters like Mabel thrived on goading other hamsters, and she would have loved it if he'd chased her. Gradually he sank down again on the floor. He felt sore and angry, at Mabel, at himself, and even at the Black Hamster. Why couldn't he have come, just for once, when Frank called, not only to give Mabel a huge shock, but to re-establish contact with Frank? How long was Frank supposed to wait? Perhaps Mabel was right, he thought sadly as he set off again towards Guy's front room. Maybe the Black Hamster had decided to move on, and call someone else. But he refused to believe that he would call Mabel. She was selfish and cruel. She had made Frank accompany her all the way back to her front room, and in the end, typically, she hadn't even thanked him. She had used him just as she used everyone else.

It was a very disgruntled hamster that made his way along the main joist to the gap beneath the fire. Frank was so put out that he didn't even pause to sniff the small but interesting objects that somehow find their way into the Spaces Between – the cotton bobbins and hair grips, the odd coin or scrap of paper. He headed straight back, feeling very dispirited and tired. All he could think about was getting back into his cage and curling up in bed. His paw hurt where he had scraped it on a sharp chip of slate.

Moodily Frank hauled himself upwards to the ledge, then paused to dust himself off. He ran his paws over his face one or two times and licked the dust off his pelt. So absorbed was he in his own thoughts that when a voice spoke behind him he leapt into the air.

'Salutations,' the voice said.

Frank wheeled round. There, instead of the Black Hamster, was a hamster with long, rather scruffy white hair and drooping whiskers. He stood on the ledge behind Frank as if he'd always been there, but Frank had failed to notice him before.

Frank gaped in astonishment and almost fell off the ledge. 'Wh-who are you?' he spluttered.

The white hamster gave a deep and rather elegant bow, with a little flourish of his right forepaw. 'I,' he said, 'am the Guardian of the Places of Power, Grand Master of the Order of the Golden Current, and Knight of Urr. But you can call me Humphrey,' he added.

3 The Knights of Urr

Frank stared at Humphrey. 'The who of the *what* – ?' he queried, not sure if he had heard him right.

Humphrey recited all his titles again. 'And your name is – ?' he said.

'What are you doing here if you don't know my name?' Frank said. He didn't mean to be rude, but this other hamster was on his territory.

'A moot point, O Nameless One,' said Humphrey. 'I came in response to your Call.'

For a moment Frank thought he meant that he had heard Frank calling from the Spaces Between, but that wasn't possible.

'I didn't call you,' he said.

'Oh, but you did,' said Humphrey, his long whiskers twitching, 'whether you realized it or not.'

Frank shook his head. He didn't like the way this strange hamster kept talking in riddles.

'What are you doing here?' he said again. 'How did you get here? And where have you come from?'

'I have come,' said Humphrey, 'from the Place of Power, along the Lines of Power, to the Receptacle of the Charge, the Magnetic Shrine.' He nodded towards the cupboard on which Frank's cage stood.

'You mean the meter cupboard?'

Humphrey lowered his voice and hissed alarmingly. 'That which you call Meter Cupboard is known to us as a Place of Power, one of the Sacred Keys to the Holy Grid – a Receptacle of –'

'All right – all right,' said Frank hastily. 'Don't start all that again. Just tell me what you want.'

'You called.'

'I didn't.'

'Your voice was heard, along the Lines of Power.'

'It can't have been,' said Frank. 'Look, I've had enough of this. I'm going to bed.'

'If the Nameless One would rest,' said Humphrey, 'then the Guardian will stand watch. That's what a Guardian does,' he added.

'Oh no you don't,' said Frank. 'You can just go back to wherever you came from. Back to your own cage.'

'I didn't come from a cage, O Nameless One,' said Humphrey. 'We of the Order eschew cages and the domination of Man.'

Frank couldn't help himself. A long shiver went up his spine and he turned around.

'Do you mean to say,' he said, 'that you don't live in a cage *at all*?'

'Of course not,' said Humphrey carelessly. 'We of the Order live and work with the Power.'

'What power?'

'The Power, O Nameless One, that will eventually set all hamsters free!'

Frank was fully awake now. His heart had quickened

and his mouth was dry. Wasn't this what he had always wanted?

'My name is Frank,' he said, and Humphrey smiled.

'Well, Frank,' he said, 'would you care to come and join us, in the Place of Power?'

Frank hesitated as Humphrey set off along the ledge. 'Where are we going?' he said. 'How long will it take to get there?'

'To get to the Portal,' said Humphrey, 'we have to go through the Magnetic Shrine.' He stopped just below Frank's cage.

'The meter cupboard,' Frank said again.

'The meter cupboard,' said Humphrey severely, 'is a Receptacle of the Force, therefore a Shrine. Have you not heard the sacred tones of the Flow?'

'Well, I have heard a funny buzzing noise,' said Frank, but Humphrey cut him short.

'Sssh,' he said. 'Listen!'

The buzzing had begun again, at a frequency that even for a hamster's sensitive hearing was almost too low, but Humphrey was listening with a rapt expression on his face.

'There is the Force that will save us all,' he murmured.

'If you say so,' said Frank doubtfully. 'But how – ?'

'Don't speak!' said Humphrey. 'Listen, and absorb. You doubt now,' he said, catching sight of the expression on Frank's face, 'but follow me, and you will experience the Force for yourself.'

'Follow you where?' said Frank.

Humphrey looked at him kindly. 'Do you not want

to meet the Knights of Urr?' he said patiently.

'Er – ?' said Frank.

'That's right,' said Humphrey. And he began to squeeze his way into the meter cupboard. Frank stared after him. He really was having the most bizarre day. Who was this hamster who spoke in riddles and looked as though he needed a good combing? Frank was wary of following him. But he could never resist an adventure, especially when he had waited patiently for so long. And it was clear that he wasn't going to get any rest in his cage.

Humphrey paused. 'Well?' he said. 'Aren't you coming?'

Frank supposed he had nothing better to do. He followed.

Inside the meter cupboard there were some black plastic boxes fixed to a panel at the back, and leading from one box to another was a thick cable. This cable ran behind the boxes, out through the panel at the back, and into the wall. Frank could see, as Humphrey began to climb the cable, that where it joined the panel behind the box there was a space just big enough for a hamster to squeeze through.

Frank's nose quivered and his whiskers twitched. Here at last was Adventure! The meter cupboard didn't look much like a shrine to him but, unless he was very much mistaken, the cable would lead outdoors and into The Wild, and Frank loved to find new ways of getting away from the houses. He followed Humphrey now, kicking with his back legs and slipping once or twice, because the cable was smooth and there were no footholds. But Frank was proud of his ability to climb, and if Humphrey could do it so could he. Humphrey was climbing easily, with both forepaws and hind paws clasping the cable on either side, and as he climbed he made a little funny noise like a continuous squeak. Frank couldn't work out where it was coming from at first, but then he realized that Humphrey was actually humming along with the cable. Frank had never heard of a hamster humming before, but it blended in so well with the other hum that after a while, intent on his difficult climb, he forgot to listen.

Humphrey's back legs kicked once, twice, then he disappeared. The part of the cable that Frank was climbing bent round and levelled out, and Frank found himself facing the small hole in the wooden panel. It was a very small hole, but hamster

bones are small too, and they can
squeeze themselves into the
tiniest gaps, which is
one reason why they
are so good at getting
away. So he pushed
and nibbled and
scrabbled and
squeezed,
thrusting
first his

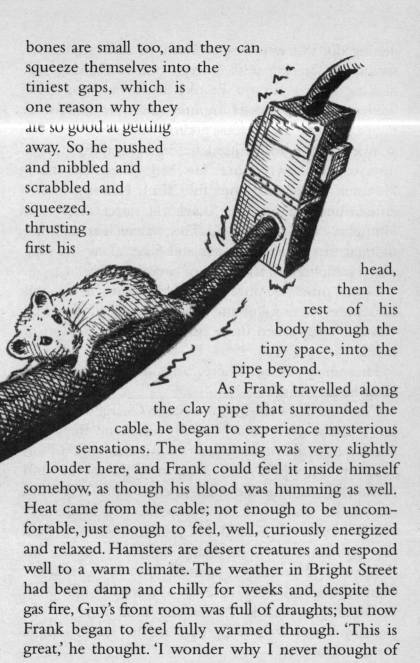

head,
then the
rest of his
body through the
tiny space, into the
pipe beyond.

As Frank travelled along
the clay pipe that surrounded the
cable, he began to experience mysterious
sensations. The humming was very slightly
louder here, and Frank could feel it inside himself
somehow, as though his blood was humming as well.
Heat came from the cable; not enough to be uncomfortable, just enough to feel, well, curiously energized
and relaxed. Hamsters are desert creatures and respond
well to a warm climate. The weather in Bright Street
had been damp and chilly for weeks and, despite the
gas fire, Guy's front room was full of draughts; but now
Frank began to feel fully warmed through. 'This is
great,' he thought. 'I wonder why I never thought of

getting out this way before.' Then, in addition, the air seemed to crackle with energy, and something was making all the fur on Frank's back stand on end. 'Perhaps this was what Humphrey meant by the Power,' Frank thought. There was certainly some strange force at work, and Frank trotted behind Humphrey, eager now to be shown more. He had called the Black Hamster, he thought, and the Black Hamster hadn't come, but maybe the Black Hamster had sent Humphrey to Frank instead. This was such an exciting thought that Frank ran faster and faster along the pipe after Humphrey, all thoughts of tiredness gone.

From time to time the cable that Frank and Humphrey were following was joined by another and when this happened there was a definite sensation of Force.

Humphrey paused. 'There, can you feel it?' he hissed. 'The Static Charge!'

Frank hadn't a clue what a Static Charge might be, but it felt marvellous. All his fur lifted and there was even a little spark flickering along the ends of his whiskers. Humphrey lifted his nose in the air and rotated it, emitting the high-pitched squeaking hum once more. And when they came to what Humphrey called the Shrine of the Holy Junction, where indeed the air did seem charged, Humphrey raised his forepaws and prostrated himself. Just for a moment Frank thought of backing away and leaving him to it, but Humphrey said, 'Come, the final stage of the journey is here. We are approaching the Sacred Temple – the Ark of Urr.'

So Frank followed Humphrey along the thickened cable as the buzzing became more distinct and increased in volume. Further and further they went, and no more cables joined the main cable, but it got warmer and noisier, until at last Frank could hardly hear himself think. As far as he could make out, they were travelling underneath The Wild itself, all the way to the other side – which was further than Frank had ever been. He could detect strange scents of wild creatures and uncultivated land, yet the pipeline itself was smooth, as if newly laid, with no useful chinks through which he might get out into The Wild. It occurred to him that it was a long way back to Guy's house.

Finally Humphrey paused, and Frank bumped into him.

'This is it,' Humphrey said. 'Our destination. The most sacred of all sacred places, Centre of the Places of Power, Generator and Transformer of the Sacred Force, Ark of the Golden Current – here we are – receive us!'

Frank tried to peer round Humphrey's shoulder, but all he could see was more pipe. He could smell a strong scent of hamster though, and more than one hamster . . . in fact it smelled like a crowd.

'Carefully now,' Humphrey said. 'To enter the Ark we must first pass through the Portal. To follow the cable further would be fatal. More than one has tried, but few have survived.'

Warily Frank followed. Humphrey hadn't said anything about 'fatal' before. But he'd come too far to back out now, so he stepped cautiously and tried to copy what Humphrey was doing. To his surprise Humphrey began to scratch on a panel of the pipe.

'It is I, Grand Master of the Knights of Urr,' he said in a low voice; and, to Frank's excitement, another voice squeaked back at him.

'Password?'

Humphrey made a noise that sounded like, 'Wirra, wirra, wirra,' and another squeak answered, 'Worra worra.'

Frank watched, fascinated, as part of the clay pipe was pulled away and Humphrey dropped silently out of the pipeline on to the floor below.

Frank hesitated, but it was too late to change his mind now. 'Get on with it,' he told himself, and he jumped away from the pipe and landed on dusty concrete a few inches below.

The first thing he noticed was that the buzzing noise was so loud that his bones vibrated with it. It seemed to come up through the concrete itself, through the underside of his paws and enter his body, a powerful low hum that from time to time skipped a beat and then began again.

The second thing he noticed was the machine that was making the humming noise: a huge metallic block with odd fixtures and attachments that Frank couldn't make out in the dark.

The third thing he noticed was a vast number of hamsters crowded on the top of the humming machine.

Frank stared in astonishment at all the hamsters, and forty or fifty pairs of hamster eyes, some ruby, but

mainly dark and glowing, peered back at Frank.

'Welcome to the Order of the Golden Current,' said Humphrey. 'Thank you, Ivor,' he added to the rather wizened, mottled hamster who had pulled the panel open for them. 'That will be all.'

Frank stared at Ivor. If Humphrey looked scruffy, this hamster was positively decrepit. He looked as if all his fur had been shaved off and stuck back on again by an enthusiastic toddler with a glue gun. In the bald bits his skin was flaking and bumpy, and Frank thought he could see boils.

'To hear is to obey, O Great One,' Ivor intoned, and he scuttled off with a hunched, lopsided gait. Frank saw that his back was crooked.

'Fellows of the Order,' declaimed Humphrey, 'Knights of Urr, tonight, at our most important ceremony, we have a very special guest. This is Frank.' He smiled at Frank, but the effect was rather like the baring of teeth. 'Frank has come at the Appointed Time, to aid us, and I know you will all welcome him.'

'Welcome, Frank,' all the hamsters chorused together, rather unnervingly, Frank thought.

'He has come at the Appointed Time, because he is the Appointed One, come for the Ceremony of Initiation, to be made a Receptacle, a living Channel for the Power.'

'The Power that Lives is the Power that Moves,' the hamsters chorused at once. 'Sacred is the Vessel, but yet more Holy is the Flow.'

'Now just hold on a minute –' said Frank.

'Prepare the wires, Ivor!' called Humphrey in a ringing voice, and with a rasp and a moan and several arthritic clicks, Humphrey began to climb up the enormous machine.

'What's going on?' said Frank. 'I've had enough of this. I'm going.' And he turned to leave, but three huge hamsters blocked his way.

'Oh, you can't leave just yet,' said Humphrey silkily. 'Not until we've explained the purpose of your visit.' And the three big hamsters moved forward.

Frank stared at them in dismay. 'What have I got myself into?' he thought. 'I'm trapped!'

4 Captured

Meanwhile, at Elsie's house, the noise had been getting worse. The family next door at number 1 played drums and electric guitar, and Elsie's cage rattled so much that once again it was in danger of falling off the shelf. Lucy thoughtfully moved the cage to the desk, though this upset the carefully arranged order in her room. She was a very neat child and had everything sorted in alphabetical order so that usually Elsie's cage stood between the toy elephant and the encyclopaedia, but now this was disrupted.

'Can't you do something, Mum?' she complained as all the cups and saucers rattled on the table.

'I'm sure they'll settle down in a bit, love,' said Angie, Lucy's mum, but then, as another picture fell off the wall, she sighed and went next door. She had to knock really loudly before she was heard.

A man opened the door. Like Sean he had a shaved head and a small tattoo on his cheek. '**WHAT CAN I DO FOR YOU, LOVE?**' he bellowed.

'Well, you could keep the nise down,' Angie said. 'These walls are thin and that guitar's very loud.'

'**THAT'LL BE SEAN,**' the man shouted. '**NO**

PROBLEM – I'LL HAVE A WORD,' and he turned and yelled up the stairs, 'OI! KEEP A LID ON IT! NEIGHBOURS CAN'T HEAR THEMSELVES THINK!'

There was a resounding chord from above and Sean's voice called downstairs, 'AWW DAD! I'M PRACTISING!'

'HE'LL PIPE DOWN NOW, LOVE,' the man shouted at Angie. 'ANYTHING ELSE I CAN DO FOR YOU?'

But Angie said no thank you, it was quite all right, and she went back to her own house and sat at the table with Lucy and Thomas in complete silence for about five minutes, until the drumming started.

BOOM da-da BOOM da-da BOOM BOOM BOOM!

'Some people!' exclaimed Lucy's mum, catching Thomas's cup before it fell on the floor.

When Les came in, he went round immediately to complain.

'Now, look,' he said. 'I'm working nights, and this time now's when I get some sleep.'

'DON'T BLAME YOU,' said Eric, Sean's dad. 'GOT TO KEEP YOUR STRENGTH UP.'

'Yes, well, I can't, can I, with all this racket going on.'

'GOTCHER, MATE,' said Eric. 'CUT IT OUT, SEAN!' he roared and the noise from above stopped abruptly.

'Right,' said Lucy's dad. 'Er – thanks.'

'ANY TIME, MATE,' bellowed Sean's dad. 'WE DON'T WANT TO GET OFF ON THE

WRONG FOOT WITH THE NEIGHBOURS

So Lucy's dad went back home and got into bed and was just settling down when there was an immensely loud vrooming noise, and the sound of furniture being bumped and banged around, and Sean's mum, Cheryl, singing at the top of her voice, 'SHAKE, RATTLE AND ROLL!'

Lucy's dad leapt out of bed. '**OI!**' he roared, almost as loudly as Sean's dad. '**WHAT'S GOING ON?**'

'Sounds like she's got the vacuum cleaner out,' said Lucy's mum, patiently stuffing cotton wool into her ears.

'THE VACUUM CLEANER?' shouted Lucy's dad. 'IT SOUNDS MORE LIKE A JUMBO JET!' And he ran round to complain once more. But it was no good. Whenever anyone complained, the new neighbours were friendly enough and kept quiet for minutes at a time, but then some new dreadful noise would begin.

'I really think they just don't know *how* to be quiet,' Angie said to Jackie, who could also hear them at number 5, and Jackie agreed. She had seen Sean's mum Cheryl in the Co-op where she worked.

'I'LL HAVE A POUND OF BACON PLEASE,' she had yelled at Jackie, though the shop was quite quiet. 'AND A FEW SLICES OF THAT NICE CORNED BEEF.'

Then she had wandered round the aisles with her shopping trolley, banging into things, so that first a stack of soup tins crashed to the floor and then she pulled over a display of baby food, and then dropped a bottle of wine, which smashed.

'**OOPS! SILLY ME**,' she boomed cheerfully at the manager. 'NEVER MIND – HAND US THAT MOP AND I'LL CLEAR IT UP!' But the manager said that she wasn't to worry, he would see to it, and would she like some help with her trolley.

'NO TA!' yelled Cheryl. 'I'LL BE FINISHED IN A TICK,' and she swung her trolley round into the videos, which cascaded down around her. Then a wheel caught in a display ribbon for the magazines and they all tumbled down as well.

'OOPS-A-DAISY! I'D BETTER GO – I'M WRECKING THE STORE!' she yelled, and she clobbered her trolley into the till. So Jackie said she thought Angie was right, it was just the way they were.

'But they're driving me mad,' Angie said. 'What's the name of that fellah who owns the house – Maruso-something? I mean, first he rents it to a weirdo like Vince, and now we've got the family from hell. I'm thinking of getting in touch with him if this carries on. You don't know where he lives, do you?'

Jackie didn't, but she said she thought it was an agency who rented the house out, and Angie could look them up in the Yellow Pages. She made Angie another coffee and they both sat at the table, looking glum. Jackie was fed up because Matchless Mick hadn't been coming round as often as usual. He'd said he could never give up life on the open road and he wanted Jackie and the boys to come with him. But Jackie was a great believer in Education.

'I don't want to take them out of school,' she said. 'And I've got my jobs to think about. It's all right for him – footloose and fancy-free – but we can't all live like that.'

'He'll want to settle down sometime, like Les,' said Angie, but Jackie said she didn't think Mick ever would.

'Mind you, Les'd have us all living on the road if it was up to him,' Angie said. 'I know he gets fed up at work. And now there's all this noise at home – well.' They both sighed as they sipped their coffee.

And of course, when the noise from number 1 died down, there was still the noise from The Wild. Lucy knew that Elsie was fretting and took her out to play and reassure her. She let Elsie look out of the window with her so that she could see what was going on.

'See, Elsie, there's a big noise, but then they just fizzle out,' she said. 'You're not in any danger.'

Elsie trembled in Lucy's palm. From where she was, the whole of The Wild seemed lit up into one big glare, with further bursts of brightness too brilliant to see.

'Mum says it's the fires that are the real problem,' Lucy went on. 'Especially for any creatures living out there – it's the smoke that's dangerous, as well as the flames. It's probably scorching them out of their hiding places right now.'

Elsie stood very still in the centre of Lucy's palm. She had a dreadful sinking feeling in her stomach. 'George,' she thought.

'Fire makes little creatures panic and run,' Lucy went on. 'Then they get lost and just run and run and run till they die. Or they just stay where they are until they get burned to death.' She kissed the top of Elsie's head wetly. 'It's a good job you don't live on the waste ground,' she said.

She put Elsie back in her cage on the desk and Elsie stayed where she was, as if paralysed herself. She could hardly breathe. 'George,' she kept thinking. It was the one clear thought in her head.

From her new position on Lucy's desk Elsie could see out of the window. She hadn't been very pleased about this – it was bad enough listening to all the explosions without having to watch them as well. But now for the first time Elsie actually tried to make out what was going on.

It wasn't easy, since hamsters are very short-sighted,

and most things further than a few inches away are a blur. They work out what's going on by using their hearing and sense of smell, which are very acute. Now when Elsie peered towards the window she thought she could make out two regular blurs of brightness among all the intermittent bursts, and her hearing told her that the group of older children invading The Wild had split into rival gangs, making bonfires at opposite ends of the heath. 'What are they doing?' Elsie thought nervously. 'Are they trying to burn down the whole croft?' And her thoughts turned again in sickening fear towards George.

There was no doubt in her mind that she would have to try to warn him. She had no clear idea of how to find him, or what they might all do once she had explained the danger. The best, indeed the only idea she had was to lead George, Daisy and her little nephews and niece back to Lucy's house, though what would happen when she got them there she didn't know. Lucy wouldn't mind, she was certain, in fact she'd be thrilled; but her parents might insist on taking them all to the pet shop, which would be disastrous. But anything was better than leaving them out there in The Wild, to be roasted to death, and already Elsie, who was a very practical hamster, was packing her pouches.

When Lucy had finally fallen asleep, Elsie began to prise the lid off her cage. She didn't do this often, since Lucy took her out regularly for exercise, so on the whole she was contented with her own little domain. But very occasionally at night when all the family were asleep, she would make her way downstairs and finish off the scraps under the kitchen table. So she knew her way around the house, though she wasn't very used to the Spaces Between. Tonight Lucy had shut her bedroom door, but her mum, who worried about fire, had, as usual, opened it just a chink before she herself had gone to bed, and Elsie was able to squeeze through.

It was a very nervous and worried hamster who made her way along the railing at the bottom of the banister, jumping and twitching at every noise: the gurgling of the cistern, the click and creak of joinery, the occasional muffled roar of a car outside. Elsie was used to all these noises, but tonight was different. Tonight, for the first time in her life, she was going to try to find her way into The Wild.

George had visited Elsie once since moving to The Wild and had brought all his little cubs to see her, so Elsie knew it was possible, somehow, to get from her house to The Wild. She had been promising herself since that day that she would visit them, but she had kept putting it off. Now, however, she was determined.

Elsie made her way across the living-room carpet to the little grid in the wall which was where she had first met George. One of the bars of the grid was broken and a cool draught blew through. Elsie climbed along the skirting board, clinging carefully to the tiny crevices, then stretched upwards and began to clamber through the cobwebbed gap. She dropped down into the dusty, musty darkness of the Spaces Between.

Sneezing because of all the dust, Elsie looked around. All her instincts were telling her to go back, but she fought them down. She knew that she didn't want to go from one house to another, she needed to get away from all the houses, and she wasn't sure how. Fleetingly she thought of Frank, who loved to explore. He would have come with her in an instant if she'd asked him, and he would know the way, but Elsie didn't want to involve Frank in such a dangerous enterprise. And neither Mabel nor Maurice would be any use. They would be getting up now and exercising or eating, safe in the comfort of their own cages. Elsie thought longingly of her own cage, and of Lucy, but she was on a mission, and if she didn't do it now she never would. Screwing up her courage, she set off in what she hoped was the direction of The Wild.

Luckily for Elsie, who would rapidly have become disorientated outside her own domain, almost the first thing she found was a trail of tiny hamster droppings, hardened in the dust. She realized immediately that these must have been left by her nephews and niece. It was almost as though they had left them specially for her, and Elsie lost no time following them, before all the strange smells and sounds and general eeriness got to her so that she couldn't move.

Elsie followed the trail of tiny droppings, not pausing, as Frank always did, to examine the small strange objects in her way: some nuts and bolts, a hairpin and a wooden dice. She couldn't wait to get away from the Spaces Between, where the air was so old and musty, and where strange things might be lurking in the dark. Unlike Frank, she didn't feel older instincts stirring and a strange, sweet thrumming of the blood, just an overwhelming desire to feel safe again. She scrabbled quickly over fragments of slate and gravel towards the outer wall of the house, and before she saw it she could smell it, a change in the air, a cool draught. There, at the bottom of the wall, was a second grid, leading directly on to the pavement. Elsie sighed in relief.

'So this is how George and the little ones got in,' she thought, and she snuffled around the outer edges of the grid, smelling all the strange smells of the pavement: tarmac and petrol, dog droppings and litter. There was a powerful smell of beer from a battered can that had rolled up against the grid; Elsie recognized the smell from when Lucy's father came home from the pub. There wasn't a single familiar, comforting smell, and almost more overpowering than the different scents was the feel of outdoor air, sharp with the promise of rain.

At one side, where the grid was attached to the wall, it was dented slightly and ill-fitting. The gap here was just a bit bigger than the gap between the bars, so Elsie began squeezing herself through from that side. She didn't dare let herself think too much about what she was doing or where she was going, or she would simply have given up. She kicked and squeezed, clinging to the sides and nibbling the mortar. Fortunately, she was a small hamster, though not quite as small as George. Mabel would never have made it, but somehow Elsie did, feeling as though she had just put herself through a very small mangle. She crawled out, on to the pavement, under the light of the single street lamp, and stayed where she was, panting and shutting her eyes against the glare. The next moment there was the roar of a car, the noise increasing to a terrifying pitch as it passed. Elsie flattened herself against the grid, trembling. Her nose was filled with the stench of petrol, her ears with a blast of music from the car radio, which was turned up loud. Elsie couldn't think, but the sound soon passed. She stayed where she was for a moment, recovering and fighting her desire to bolt back the way she had come.

'It's all right,' she told herself. She knew about cars and had known that she would have to face traffic. She was very near The Wild now, all she had to do was open her eyes and continue. 'You've come this far,' she told herself severely as though speaking to George. 'You can't go back.' Cautiously she prised herself away from the grid. 'You have to open your eyes,' she said to herself. 'Come on, the worst is over now.'

Unfortunately for Elsie, this wasn't true. She opened her eyes and wished immediately that she hadn't. The smell of car in her nostrils was replaced by something even more unpleasant: something sharp, pungent and animal. Cats.

To Elsie's blurred vision it looked as though there were hundreds of them in all directions, and the two biggest ones, nearest her, were crouched in a stalking position, tails twitching, and their eyes, lit terrifyingly by the street lamp, intent on Elsie.

For a moment no one moved. Elsie's first thought was that she had failed, because now she would never reach The Wild to warn George. Her second thought was that she hoped it would be over quickly, and that Lucy wouldn't be too upset. Her third thought was that no one was moving, and she should really try to make a dash for it. She felt all the muscles in her body tense, ready to run.

At the same time the nearest cat leapt. She found herself looking at the snowy underside of his body, the pink paw pads. With a yowl the second cat sprang also, then the first cat descended. She felt a blast of cat breath, then sharp teeth at the back of her neck, and she sank into a dizzying darkness, in the grip of the first cat's jaws.

5 The Rite of Power

Frank stared at the three huge hamsters. The biggest of all had only one eye, which gave him a villainous look, as though he would fight hard and well. Frank wondered which one to take on first, and how long he would last in a fight, but then Humphrey spoke.

'Gentlemen please,' he said in his silky tones. 'This is our honoured guest. Escort him to the altar.'

The three hamsters surrounded Frank. 'Courage!' he thought, and he reared into his most threatening pose.

'Step back,' he said. 'And step back now.'

'Frank,' drawled Humphrey, 'you've come all this way. Surely you want to see us perform the Rite of Power.'

'I don't think so,' Frank said. 'I'm going back.'

'Oh, but you can't go back, not just yet,' said Humphrey. 'Everyone here, in the Ark of Urr, has assembled in your honour. We're all waiting for you.'

'I don't know what you're talking about,' said Frank. 'What on earth do you mean?'

Humphrey's eyes glowed. 'It was no accident that I found you, Frank,' he said, and eerily behind him all the hamsters started to hum. 'Your fame has spread – all the way from the pet shop to The Wild.'

Frank shook his head to clear it from the sound of humming. 'What do you mean?' he said again.

'Are you not the same Frank who charted the depths of the Unknown Kingdom of the Sewers?' said Humphrey. 'And fought the unholy rats therein? Are you not he who –' and here Humphrey's voice sank to a whisper, 'speaks to the Nameless One – of Narkiz?'

About a hundred questions surged into Frank's mind. How did Humphrey know all this, and what else did he know about Narkiz, and the Black Hamster? Why had Humphrey brought him here? He started to speak, then stopped. He closed his mouth, then opened it again, as one question fought its way to the surface.

'If you knew who I was,' he said, 'how come you didn't know my name?'

'Oh, I knew your name, Frank,' said Humphrey smoothly. 'I just needed you to confirm it.'

Curiosity and confusion battled in Frank, but curiosity won. 'What *is* all this?' he said, waving a paw.

Humphrey nodded approvingly. 'You have a right to know, Frank,' he said. 'But I can't tell you – I can only show you. Won't you come with me?'

Feeling as though he had stumbled into a dream, Frank allowed himself to be led upwards from one ledge to another, ascending the side of the huge, vibrating machine. There were all kinds of bumps and ridges, ledges and cables, and Humphrey ascended slowly, with Frank behind him and the three big hamsters bringing up the rear. It was rather like climbing a mountain, except that all the time Frank felt a peculiar charge, like a current of energy, coming from the great machine. Frank noticed all Humphrey's fur was standing on end. There was a lot of it so that he looked like a ball of angora wool that was about to unravel. Frank felt his own fur lifting and a curious, heady feeling gripping him as he climbed.

They passed a row of hamsters gathered together on a ledge roughly halfway up the machine and humming continuously in time to the vibrations coming from it.

'Behold, the Knights of the Outer Circle,' said Humphrey. Frank stared at the hamsters. Their eyes were blank and glassy, intent on their tuneless hum, and, one way or another, they all looked, well, damaged. Some had one eye, others one ear, or a club paw; but there was no time to ask questions, and he needed all his breath for climbing.

Further on, they came to another ledge where more hamsters were gathered, humming.

'Behold, the Middle Circle,' said Humphrey. He seemed a little out of breath himself and didn't elaborate on this, and Frank certainly had no breath left; but these hamsters were, if possible, even tattier than the first set.

At last Humphrey reached the top and, extending a paw to Frank, hauled him over the edge. Exhausted by his climb, for a moment he didn't take in the view around him.

'Behold,' panted Humphrey.

The top surface of the great machine was entirely flat, level and smooth. More hamsters were gathered there, balding, mangy, lame, with various bits missing.

The noise of humming here was so loud that Frank felt as though fingernails were scraping the inside of his skull. But, as Frank approached, the hamsters parted, creating a kind of path. And as they parted, Frank could see that there, in the centre of the great plateau, was a large and curious structure, like a great triangle or pyramid, made up of many ledges, small planks and fragments of slate. The whole building was the height of many hamsters, and there was an entrance into it large enough for a hamster to pass through.

Frank was speechless, but beside him Humphrey seemed possessed by a curious excitement.

'Behold the Ziggurat of Urr!' he cried.

'Urrrrrrrrr,' said all the hamsters, exactly imitating the whirring of the great machine.

Frank stared, first at the strange building, then away in the direction he had just climbed. He hadn't appreciated before just how many hamsters there were, gathered at different points of the machine, but now all he could see were hamsters of all kinds and colours, and varieties of damage, clustering up the sides. He felt a peculiar light-headedness, as though he had in fact climbed a great mountain, and could see a whole nation of hamsters before him – just as before, with the Black Hamster, he had seen the whole of the hamster tribe. And all these hamsters were gazing at Frank, their fur lifted like his, and shifting from one foot to another as they maintained their peculiar, whirring hum. It made it difficult to think.

'Wh-who are all these hamsters?' he asked. 'Where have they all come from? And what's the matter with them?' he added.

Humphrey regarded Frank with satisfaction.

'They come from many places,' he said. 'From cages in the human world they made their own way here, called by the lure of that Shrine you call Meter Cupboard. Most suffered terribly in the human world. Some were considered faulty, and were abandoned. But now this is their home – we live, and worship here. We are Servants of the Power.'

'You mean – you all *live* here?' Frank whispered. 'But how – how do you eat – what do you do?'

'We follow the Paths of Power,' Humphrey said, 'and they bring us to the Places of Food. Those in the Outer Circle forage for the rest. In the Middle and Inner Circles we maintain the Hum.'

'Hmm –' said Frank doubtfully.

'That's right,' said Humphrey, darting swiftly to Frank's side and speaking close into his ear. 'By humming constantly we attune ourselves to the Flow of Power, and this in turn tunes us in to higher levels of consciousness. Higher and higher we raise our awareness, until we can enter the Unmanifest Zones, and communicate directly with Him.'

Frank shook his head again. 'With who?' he asked.

'With the Nameless One!' cried Humphrey.

'The Power that Lives is the Power that Gives,' all the hamsters chorused. 'Sacred is the Vessel but yet more Holy is the Flow.'

Frank struggled to get a grip on his thoughts. 'But what are you trying to *do*?' he said.

'That is what I must explain to you,' said Humphrey.

He darted forward again, so that he was very close to Frank and his whiskers tickled Frank's ears. 'But not here,' he said in a low voice. 'What I have to say is not for all ears.' He looked round swiftly to left and right. 'I want to show you the Sacred Tabernacle,' he said more loudly. 'Won't you come in.'

Wordlessly, Frank followed. Hamsters drew away from him as he went, all the time maintaining their curious, toneless hum. When he glanced directly at a hamster, Frank felt a little sick. They seemed turned in on themselves somehow, unfocused. It was as though behind the eyes no one was in.

Humphrey stopped at the entrance of the strange building. Ivor hobbled forward. He held a strand of red ribbon out to Humphrey, who draped it ostentatiously across his own shoulders.

'Worra worra worra,' he muttered, rolling his eyes back in his head, and then he spoke some other strange words that sounded to Frank like the munching of hamster food. Then, with a quick sideways look at Frank, he made several weird gestures with his paws.

Finally he turned to Frank, paws raised. 'The Force grants us access,' he said. 'After you.'

But even though Frank was finding it increasingly difficult to think clearly, he wasn't going to enter that strange structure alone. They might shut the door behind him and seal him in. So he shook his head again and said, 'No, after you.'

Humphrey smiled as though he guessed what Frank was thinking, but he said, 'As you wish,' and walked ahead of Frank with stately, rhythmical movements, and all around the ziggurat the hamsters prostrated themselves and the note of their humming changed.

Frank followed Humphrey, still feeling as if he was in a dream. Inside, the Force struck him with even greater intensity, the humming, whirring noise seemed magnified, his fur lifted even further and the ends of his whiskers crackled. There was no doubt that there was a force at work here, a definite power, whatever it was.

In the gloom of the ziggurat Frank could make out a large stone and what looked like – and in fact was – a mousetrap. A cable lay at either end of this mousetrap, the copper wires glinting dully.

'This is the altar of Urr,' Humphrey said in Frank's ear, making him jump.

Frank glanced at Humphrey and saw to his surprise that he was carrying a toothpick as a kind of sceptre.

'The Knights of Urr number thirteen in all,' he murmured, 'with myself as Grand Master. We alone designed this place, setting the other followers to work. No detail was overlooked; lives were lost, but in the end we succeeded. This is the place where The Force can communicate directly with us, through the power of vision. Behold the Seat of Seeing!'

He pointed to the stone.

'What do you mean, "communicate directly"?' Frank said slowly.

'Vision,' said Humphrey. 'That's how the knowledge is imparted – through visions of the way things could be – will be – when all hamsters are free. But to tell you of these things is nothing, Frank – you have to take the seat.'

Frank eyed the stone doubtfully.

Seeing the expression on his face, Humphrey said, 'It is there, and only there, that you can communicate with the Nameless One of Narkiz.'

A thrill shivered up Frank's spine. Wasn't this what he had longed for?

'Call Him, Frank,' said Humphrey urgently. 'Listen to the knowledge He imparts. He will communicate with you, as He never has before. He has been waiting, Frank, for you to summon Him.'

'But I don't summon him,' Frank said. 'He just – appears.'

'Frank,' said Humphrey solemnly, 'you are the Vessel. It is through you that He appears.'

This was a new thought to Frank, and he wasn't entirely sure about it. But before he could open his mouth to object, Humphrey said, 'Let me show you something,' and he pushed the ends of the cable

towards the steel bar of the mousetrap. Instantly there was a flash of blue light and sparks appeared. 'That is what the Force can do,' said Humphrey. 'We could be a free nation again, Frank, free from human rule, serving only Him. That's why we've brought you here – you are the Appointed One, come at the Appointed Time!'

A mixture of thoughts and emotions battled in Frank. All these hamsters, gathered and waiting to become a free nation – that was what he had dreamed of for so long. Yet all this Inner and Outer Circle business, and the chanting, and worshipping the Force – he wasn't sure about all that. But he had waited for so long and nothing had happened. Maybe, just maybe, Humphrey was right, and he did have to summon the Black Hamster, to show him that these other hamsters were ready and waiting for him to take them to Narkiz.

Humphrey watched as hope and desire flitted across Frank's face, waging a battle with doubt. Then, before doubt could win, he said, 'Won't you at least try the Seat of Seeing?'

Frank swallowed, but he couldn't resist. Humphrey held out his paw to the stone, and wordlessly Frank climbed on top. He opened his mouth to say 'What now?' but suddenly there was the flash of blue light again, and he was overwhelmed by a surprising giddiness. He felt all at once as if he was at a great height, as if he was standing on a mountain. Every strand of fur on his body seemed charged with a peculiar force, and he could see flickering images in his mind.

'Hold the vision, Frank!' Humphrey cried shrilly from below. 'Bring it into focus, into the centre of your mind's eye!'

Frank struggled to do as he was told, but the flickering images gathered force and momentum until he seemed to be at the centre of a whirlwind, through which he could hear only Humphrey's chanting, and the buzzing of the machine.

Then slowly, in the centre of his vision, a single image began to resolve and grow. Frank saw that he was indeed on a mountain, and that below him, stretching in all directions as far as the eye could see, was a vast plain. It was a desolate plain, not exactly a desert, but featureless and composed mainly of bald patches of earth. The grass that had once been there was withered and scorched. It was as though Frank was looking at a bare and barren version of The Wild – an image of The Wild grown huge and devoid of life.

'What do you see, Frank?' Humphrey's voice spoke unnervingly close to him, almost as though he was somehow inside Frank's head.

Frank didn't want to answer, but he said, 'I see a big, deserted place, like The Wild, only bigger – no plants, no trees, nothing.'

'That's it!' Humphrey said excitedly. 'That's the New Kingdom!'

It didn't look like much of a kingdom, Frank thought. He was looking at the sky above the bare heath. Great pewter-coloured clouds were gathering, and it seemed to Frank that he could see all this in unnatural detail. Frank was as short-sighted as the rest of his race and was not usually able to see so far, or so clearly. 'What's happening?' he thought.

'It may look barren now,' Humphrey's voice was saying, 'but we can change all that, Frank, with His help.'

Frank stopped looking at the sky, and instead angled his new-found vision as far as possible over the heath, miles and miles, he thought, to the horizon. But everywhere he looked was empty and desolate. Where was the Black Hamster, if this was his new domain?

'Call Him, Frank,' Humphrey's voice whispered. 'Call Him, and He'll come.'

But Frank hesitated, unsure. The Black Hamster usually came in his own time, when he was needed, and he was the one who did the calling.

'Throw yourself off the mountain,' Humphrey's voice whispered on, 'and He will catch you.' For a moment Frank had a dizzying sensation of falling, then the sensation of being caught, held safe, by the hamster he most wanted to see. He put out a paw and felt the reassuring stone. 'None of this is happening,' he thought. But Humphrey's voice still spoke to him.

'All this could be ours, Frank, yours and mine – a Kingdom of Hamsters away from the rule of men – a New Narkiz!'

And suddenly, everywhere Frank looked was swarming with life – it looked as if the heath itself had suddenly started crawling, but it was crawling with hamsters. Everywhere, as far as Frank could see, the heath was alive with hamsters of every colour and variety, and they were all running towards the mountain on which Frank stood.

'All you have to do is call Him, Frank,' murmured Humphrey. 'Call Him, and the hamster race is saved –'

As Frank scanned the swarming crowd he thought he saw faces he recognized: George and Daisy, Chestnut and, behind them, Elsie, then Felicity with Drew.

'– no longer will cubs be taken from their dams, bought and sold into slavery –'

And suddenly there was a little clearing in the swarming crowd, and in the centre of it was a beautiful grey-white hamster whose coat had a satin sheen. 'Leila,' Frank breathed. It was his dam.

Frank had seen her only once before, in a shared memory with Chestnut, but the image of her had haunted him ever since. Now here she was, gazing up at Frank with all the love and adoration that a cub might desire. Tears sprang into Frank's eyes. He wanted to run down from the mountain towards her, but already the little space in the milling crowd was filling up again with hamsters, and he could no longer see the fine, silvery face. 'Leila!' he cried. And all at once he was sliding down from the mound, his visions flickering before him. It was over.

Frank lay, wedged between the mousetrap and the Seat of Seeing. Humphrey's white, whiskery face loomed over him anxiously.

'Did you see Him?' he said urgently. 'Was He there?'

'Who?' said Frank stupidly.

'The Nameless One, of course!' cried Humphrey. 'The Nameless One of Narkiz!'

Frank got up stiffly. 'If you mean the Black Hamster,' he said, 'then no, he wasn't. He was about the only one who wasn't there.'

Humphrey clutched him in excitement. 'But did you Call Him, Frank?' he cried. 'Did you try?'

Frank shook his head in an attempt to clear it. There was a peculiar throbbing sensation all over his body.

'No, I didn't try,' he said, rubbing his forehead. 'I was too busy seeing – all the other things.' For a moment he had nearly said 'Leila', and he thought of her now with a pang. What had he just seen? Was any of it true?

Humphrey clutched his pelt even harder. 'But you were supposed to try,' he said in a peculiar, strained voice. 'That's why I brought you here.'

Frank shook Humphrey off. 'Now just hold on a minute,' he said. 'Why exactly do you want me to summon the Black Hamster?'

Humphrey's face was ugly with greed. 'Why else?' he shrieked. 'Only the Nameless One can lead us to the New Narkiz. Did you not see it, Frank? A vast stretch of land populated only by hamsters – free from the human vermin – and we can rule them, Frank, you and I – a kingdom of hamsters, ruled in peace. But the Nameless One has to speak through you, Frank.'

Humphrey put his hand on Frank's pelt and again Frank shook him off.

'You're mad,' he said.

'Think of it,' Humphrey breathed, 'King of your own Kingdom.'

'I don't want to be king,' Frank said.

'A republic then,' urged Humphrey. 'A Republic of Hamsters – free from Man, free from Predators – all the hamsters in the world gathered in their own territory – the way it used to be.'

Frank hesitated, doubts struggling in his mind. It was hard to argue with Humphrey, but he did somehow feel that none of this was right.

'If you rule over hamsters,' he said, 'how can they be free?'

Humphrey shook his head impatiently. 'All tribes need leaders,' he said. 'They need wisdom and guidance. You can't just lead hamsters into the wild and leave them there – they'll run amok and be preyed upon. No – any great movement needs leaders.'

Frank still wasn't convinced. 'I don't know,' he said.

'The visions, Frank,' said Humphrey, and there was a pale light in his eyes. 'Night after night I fasted and remained in here until the mystery of our race was revealed to me – the new direction we must take to restore ourselves to our former glory. It wasn't easy, but someone had to do it – for the sake of the Tribe. You can do it too, Frank. If you stay in here and fast, it will all be shown to you.'

Frank wasn't sure that he liked the idea of this. 'I think I'd rather go home, if it's all the same to you,' he said.

'Go home?' said Humphrey. 'What is *home*?'

Frank couldn't answer this. He thought of Guy, then he thought of Narkiz.

'Go home – and then what?' said Humphrey, pacing rapidly up and down. 'Return to your cage? How far has that got you? Or have you got another plan to free our tribe?'

Frank hadn't, of course. He still had no idea what the Black Hamster had meant when he had said, 'Help my people.' Maybe, just maybe, Humphrey was right, and drastic steps had to be taken. But he still didn't like the way Humphrey was looking at him.

'Perhaps I don't have a plan,' he said, looking Humphrey in the eye. 'But neither do you. You don't know, any more than I do, how to lead hamsters to their own territory.'

'No,' said Humphrey, and there was a peculiar note of triumph in his voice. 'But you can contact the One who Knows, Frank. You can summon Him and bring Him here, and He can tell us. That's why I brought you here, Frank. This is the place. The hamster tribe awaits. Summon Him, Frank, and He will tell us what to do.'

'And suppose I don't want to?' said Frank.

Humphrey smiled, and it was not a pleasant smile. He stood between Frank and the door.

'Then,' he said, 'you will stay here until you do.' And before Frank could move, he had whisked himself outside the ziggurat and something large and heavy was being rolled across the entrance. Frank ran up to it at once, but the three big hamsters had already heaved a large stone across the doorway. Frank pushed at it with all his might, but it didn't budge.

'*Oi!*' he cried.

'Don't try to escape, Frank.' Humphrey's voice came smoothly through a chink at the top of the stone. 'We're all waiting for you here. And waiting for Him. You can come out when you bring Him with you!'

Frank pushed and hammered against the stone.

'You're crazy, all of you!' he shouted. 'Let me out!'

6 The Jaws of Death

Elsie didn't faint, though she very much wished she could. She felt herself slacken and grow limp, as though she was a cub being carried by its mum. Sharp teeth bit into the loose flesh at the back of her neck, she could feel moisture from the cat's mouth dribbling into her fur and its hot, moist breath around her ears. He had picked her up and was trotting along the street with her dangling from his jaws like a scrap of meat, all the other cats trotting silently behind. The pavement lurched and bobbed about beneath her until she felt sick and closed her eyes.

'Where are they taking me?' she thought. 'Why don't they just kill me now?'

Something told her that this was what cats did: they played with you first. She tried hard not to think about this and she wished fervently that she had stayed in her cage, but there was no point thinking that either. She just had to face her death when the time came, like thousands of other creatures before her.

Then the swaying motion stopped, and a different motion took its place. Elsie's eyes peeped open. The cat was pushing his way through a little door at the bottom of a big door – a cat flap, Elsie thought with dull surprise, and she realized that he must be taking her inside Mrs Timms's house, because Mrs Timms was the only person in the street who had a cat flap. She fed all the cats for miles around, putting out cat food on saucers.

With a push and a squeeze the big cat entered and trotted across the linoleum on Mrs Timms's floor. Elsie heard the cat flap open and close behind them several times as the other cats followed. The whole house smelled very strongly of litter and cat wee – though, Elsie thought mournfully, a bad smell was the least of her problems. Now that her eyes were open she could see all the saucers of cat food scattered around the floor. 'Typical,' she thought bitterly. These cats weren't even hungry. They were going to kill her for fun.

Then the big cat spoke out of the corner of his mouth. 'Right, chaps,' he said, 'gather round. We'll play the game fair and square. I'll put the little fellah down, and first one to pounce wins, OK?'

There was a lot of grumbling from the other cats at this.

'Not again!'

'You always win!'

'Why don't we just divide it up between us?'

'I caught it, didn't I?' said the big cat aggressively. 'And if I says we're playing the game, then we play. Or I could just take it off and eat it all by myself.'

Gradually the grumbling died down and the cats formed a circle around the big cat. Then Elsie felt herself being lowered with extreme gentleness to the floor, which was covered in the same kind of oilcloth as the hallway. 'No carpet,' she thought – at the same time thinking that this was hardly the moment to be noticing the décor.

'Now get ready,' said the big cat, 'and when I give the word, pounce. On three. One –'

Elsie shut her eyes tightly.

'Two –'

She knew she should at least try to run, but her legs seemed to be paralysed. It was like the beginning of death.

'And thr–'

Suddenly, without warning, all the lights clicked on, and a voice said shrilly, 'Alfie, Stinker, Minx – what are you doing?'

It was Mrs Timms who, unable to sleep that night, had come downstairs to pour herself another strong drink. Now she grabbed the tall broom that stood by the door and made sweeping movements at the cats, a little unsteadily, since she had already had rather too much to drink.

The cats scattered as she shooed them, calling them terrible names. 'A naughty boy you are,' she scolded. 'No mice, no mice – I told you!'

Alfie cowered behind a kitchen chair.

'Anyone would think I didn't feed you,' she grumbled, still sweeping away at the fleeing cats. 'If this carries on, no more food – do you hear?'

By now, all the cats were skulking behind the furniture, tails twitching, looking aggrieved.

'Now then,' said Mrs Timms. 'What is it – what is it

here?' And she bent down rather unsteadily towards Elsie, who still cowered in the middle of the floor, unable to think where to run, or even how to run. Mrs Timms's hands cupped her, then she was lifted gently up. Elsie curled tightly into a ball. She was used to being picked up by humans, of course, but never by a human who smelled like this. Mrs Timms gave off the sour smell of cat wee, alcohol and unwashed human; there were stains all down the front of her nightgown. She burped as she lifted Elsie towards her face and the smelly blast was overwhelming.

'Pardon,' she said, pronouncing her words very carefully. 'Now then – not a mouse at all, are you, my pretty one? Well – what are you?' She lifted Elsie up to the light, which of course made Elsie squirm even further into a ball. 'I don't know what you are,' said Mrs Timms, squinting. 'But never worry. You're safe now, my pretty pet, but where to put you?' And she carried Elsie around the different objects in the room, of which there were an unusual number, mumbling to herself.

'Not the cat basket – a drawer maybe? – no, teapot? – no – where shall we put you, eh?'

And then her eye fell on a tall spindly object in the corner of the room.

'Oh yes,' she said. 'Oh, just the place – just the place for you.'

And she carried Elsie over to the spindly thing, from which a kind of cage dangled. A birdcage.

'My poor little Bobby lived here,' she told Elsie as she opened a door in the front of the cage and released

Elsie into it. 'In there he'd sit and sing and sing.' She closed the door. 'Maybe you'll give me a little song too, when you're feeling better, eh?' She beamed at Elsie with her big watery eyes and poked a finger through the bars of the cage. 'Who's a pretty boy then?' she said. 'I'm going to call you Bobby.'

But Elsie didn't like the dangling cage at all. She was used to her cage having a solid floor on which she could run around. Now she clung to the bars at the base of this cage, which rocked dangerously whenever she tried to move. The floor seemed miles away, and from it several pairs of cats' eyes glared up at her with intent.

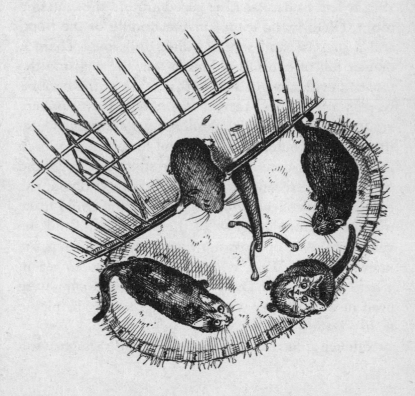

'I'm not a bird,' she told Mrs Timms. 'I'm a hamster! Don't leave me in here, please.'

But of course Mrs Timms couldn't hear her. She went on clucking and whistling at Elsie for a while, then she turned to the cats.

'Come on now, Stinker, Lurch,' she said. 'Eat up, then out you go – but no hunting, do you hear?'

She opened the door and prodded the nearest cat out, and reluctantly the others followed.

'Safe now, Bobby,' she said to Elsie as she went out. 'And in the morning I'll fetch some lovely bird seed.'

'No!' cried Elsie, rattling the bars of her cage so that it swung horribly. 'Come back!' But Mrs Timms had already left. In despair Elsie gazed around the cluttered room. There was a teapot in the middle of the floor, and a suitcase, and several china dolls on a chair. A drawer full of cotton bobbins lay on the rug, and the cats had evidently got at it so that some of the bobbins were scattered and thread was tangled everywhere around the furniture. The birdcage stood on its own so that the cats couldn't climb up the furniture and reach it, which was some comfort, Elsie supposed, but it did of course also mean that she couldn't climb down. She could see out of the window, though. She could make out the soft orange glow of the street lamp, and the yellowish beam of a passing car. Beyond the lamp, she knew, was The Wild, which she had failed to reach, where George and Daisy and all the little cubs were even now in danger while she, Elsie, swung helplessly from a birdcage.

'Oh why did I ever leave Lucy?' she thought. And

why did Frank enjoy getting out so much, when all it led to was horrible danger? She had to escape, she simply had to – but how? The floor was a dizzying distance away, and there were all the cats. Elsie gazed at the window, clutching the bars of the cage. 'Somebody help me,' she squeaked faintly, then louder, 'Help me, someone, please. Help! Help!'

Hours passed and Bright Street gradually woke up. But it was the half-term holiday and the children weren't up early as usual, or at least, if they were, they weren't out. Jake and Josh sat in their pyjamas watching TV and eating cornflakes, Tania was still in bed (she always liked to lie in until 10.30 in the holidays) and Thomas was up, but was playing on his games console. At around 8.30 Lucy stirred restlessly in bed, then she sat up, and the first thing she noticed was that the lid of Elsie's cage was open, and Elsie was gone. From then on number 3 Bright Street was in uproar as Lucy ran around shouting, 'Mum! Dad! Elsie's gone!' She ran up to Thomas's room in the attic and yelled at him, 'You've taken her, haven't you? WHERE'S MY HAMSTER!'

'I HAVEN'T SEEN YOUR OLD HAMSTER!' Thomas yelled back.

'Lucy – Thomas – what is it?' Lucy's mum called up the stairs.

'THOMAS HAS TAKEN ELSIE!' shouted Lucy.

'**I HAVEN'T!**' bellowed Thomas, and so it went on, and all morning they hunted for Elsie, behind furniture and at the backs of cupboards. But of course it would never occur to them that she was in a bird-cage in Mrs Timms's front room.

As the morning drew on, the older boys and girls began to gather on The Wild. Some brought planks of wood and cardboard boxes to add to the great piles that would be bonfires in a few days' time. There were two of them, one at either end, and the boys and girls had split roughly into two rival gangs. They heckled each other from opposite ends of the waste ground.

'We'll burn you out! We'll burn you out!'

'Yah! You couldn't burn out a match!'

'Oh yeah? Well, you couldn't light a match!' And the bonfires grew huge as the two gangs worked furiously to outdo each other.

'I don't know where those kids get their money from,' Arthur said, watching them from his window. 'But those fireworks aren't cheap.'

From Mrs Timms's window Elsie watched them in an agony of worry. Would George be safe, once both bonfires were lit and all the fireworks were exploding? She was stiff and uncomfortable after a night in the birdcage, and she felt even worse when Lucy walked right past the window, to call for Tania. The two of them walked past again and Elsie rattled the bars of her cage furiously.

'I can't find her anywhere,' Lucy was saying. 'We've looked in all the cupboards and everywhere.'

'Lucy, *Lucy*!' Elsie squeaked. 'I'm here!'

Tania put her arm through Lucy's.

'She can't have got very far,' she said. 'I'll help you look.'

'Here I am,' squeaked Elsie. 'Oh, do look round!'

But Tania and Lucy walked by.

Meanwhile Sean had got up and was loitering outside the noisy house. He heckled the two girls as they approached. 'Eh, Plaits! Fatso! Want to see what I've got?'

'Ignore him,' Lucy said witheringly as she let herself in.

'Boys are so immature,' said Tania.

The truth was that Sean was bored. He was a bit aggressive with other children and wasn't finding it easy to make friends. But today was different. He had talked an older boy into buying some fireworks for him, and he was going to take them to one of the gangs. He strolled casually over to the nearest bonfire.

'Push off,' said one of the older boys, who had a big, meaty face.

'Can't I watch?' said Sean.

''S not for littl'uns,' said the big boy.

'I'm thirteen,' said Sean, who was nearly eleven.

'So?' said the big boy. 'Push off back to your mum.'

'I can watch if I like,' said Sean.

There might have been an argument, but then one of the other boys, who had a long thin face and a big jaw, said, 'Where'd you get your chain from?' He was looking at the chain that ran from Sean's left ear to his nostril.

'Did it myself,' said Sean. 'With a skewer!'

'You never,' said the older boy, and all the boys gathered round. Sean explained to them how he'd heated the skewer then plunged it into his ear, and his mum had gone mad because she could smell the burning flesh. This was all quite untrue, since, after weeks of begging, his mother had finally taken him to a shop, where they'd done it properly; but the older boys looked impressed. They called him Punk and said he could help them build the bonfire if he liked.

'I can do better than that,' Sean said, and he unzipped his jacket and pulled out the fireworks, and his dad's silver lighter. The older boys whistled and jeered and clapped.

'All right – you're in,' said the meaty-faced one. 'But you've got to work. Our bonfire's got to be bigger than theirs, and we want the most explosions, right? We're gonna blast them out!'

Sean was happy, working with the older lads, all of whom had names like Spadge and Bexy. He felt as though he was part of a team, even though they made him do most of the fetching and carrying. Their main job seemed to be shouting names at the other gang. Sean knew where there was a skip, and he dragged a broken chair from it and a window frame. When he got back, all the lads had gathered round Bexy, the thin-faced boy with the big jaw.

'Go on – I dare ya!'

'Bite its head off!'

Sean pushed in through the huddle of boys. Bexy had a mouse by its tail. It wriggled and kicked, turning slowly round in mid-air. Bexy raised it high and opened his mouth. All the boys started chanting, 'In – In – In – In!'

Sean felt a bit sick, but he had to watch. Higher and

higher Bexy held the wriggling mouse, and he opened his mouth wider than Sean had known a mouth could be opened. Then, all at once, he dropped the mouse and shut his mouth like a trap. Sean shut his eyes. The lads jeered and groaned and made gagging noises, then they all started laughing. Sean opened his eyes just in time to see the mouse scuttling away across his foot.

'Had you fooled there, littl'un,' Bexy said, grinning, and Spadge asked Sean if he wanted a bag to be sick in.

'Shut your mouth,' said Combo, the boy with the big meaty face, chucking Sean under the chin. 'A mouse might fall in!' And all the boys roared with laughter.

Sean felt shown up. 'I don't feel sick!' he said. 'I've eaten a rat before now!'

Catcalls and jeers from the gang.

'I *have*!' shouted Sean. 'Ask anyone!'

'Well – maybe we should find him one then!' said Combo, and the others agreed.

Before Sean knew what was happening, they were jostling him towards a clump of withered bushes. When he looked at the earth around the bushes he could see that it was full of tiny holes. Combo, Bexy and Spadge prodded and poked with long sticks into the holes and around the bushes but, much to Sean's relief, there were no further sightings of small animals.

'You have to wait a bit, sometimes,' Spadge said.

Now, even though Sean had no desire at all to eat a live rat, he did feel that he had to save face somehow, in front of the gang. He too found a stick and began to poke around, then suddenly he had a wicked idea.

'We could smoke them out!' he said. 'Light the fireworks, and stick them into the holes!'

Everyone thought this was a brilliant idea, and Sean began to feel restored to his former glory as a gang member.

'Who's gonna light them?' said Spadge.

'I will,' said Sean, and he withdrew his dad's lighter from his inside pocket.

I don't need to tell you that Sean was being very foolish. Even Thomas, Jake and Josh knew how dangerous fireworks were, and that only an adult should handle them. But it seemed that, once he had started, Sean just couldn't stop showing off. He couldn't look as though he was nervous of lighting explosive material, even though, just for a second, the horrible images of burned arms and faces that he'd seen on films flashed through his mind. He took the long thin fireworks, lit the end with his dad's lighter, and then, ignoring every safety instruction on the packet, thrust the smoking end into the holes in the ground.

Some of the fireworks sputtered and went out. But some ripped into the ground, blasting through it like gunpowder and making loud, satisfying reports like a gun. Little fountains of earth shot up through the holes and small mounds appeared, like the mounds made by moles. Each time this happened, all the gang cheered, and Sean began to walk with a bit of a swagger. Soon everyone wanted a go, and the air was filled with burning, caustic fumes.

Beneath the ground there was terrible consternation. Cries and squeaks and squeals came from all directions, from the wounded, the trapped, the lost. Little fieldmice, voles and shrews scurried in all directions, calling to their young, and were blocked by sudden falls of earth, or overcome by burning smoke. Some collapsed, deafened by the blast, and at least two little mice were burned alive. Only the worms and beetles were able to scurry and slither away through the sliding earth and showers of small stones.

'What is it? What is it?' cried the little fieldmice, panicking. 'Is it the end of the world?'

Poking his head out of his burrow, Capper Fieldmouse watched the chaos in bewilderment, then he pulled one or two of the smaller shrews to safety as more earth collapsed behind them. 'What's going on?' he demanded, but the shrews were too dazed and in shock to reply.

Everywhere there was moaning and lamentations, and the terrible smell of scorched earth and burning fur.

'It's those dreadful boys again,' he said to himself with a shudder, remembering the awful sight of Bexy's open jaws. Yes, in fact it was Capper who had been caught by Bexy and, released, had run across Sean's foot. He had retreated to his burrow in order to recover, but now it looked as though his burrow would be lost.

'Can't stay here, that's for sure,' he said to the trembling shrews. 'Have to warn the others.' The thought of George and Daisy and the little cubs flashed through his mind. 'Have to dig,' he said hoarsely to the shrews. 'Dig and burrow, dig and burrow – come on –

get on with it!' and he hurled himself at the back wall of his burrow, tunnelling furiously.

Meanwhile, in their burrow, George and Daisy could also hear the commotion.

'Whatever's going on?' said Daisy after a particularly loud eruption. All the little hamsters huddled together, for once forgetting to fight. George picked up little Elsie.

'It's probably just those daft lads again,' he said, more cheerfully than he felt, but then another blast rocked the burrow. 'It's just the fireworks,' he called to Daisy, who had crouched over the boys.

'What *are* they doing with them?' she said when the earth had stopped falling, but George didn't know.

There was another ripping, tearing noise, then a series of blasts, shaking the burrow again. All the little hamsters burrowed under George and Daisy, and they looked at each other with worried faces.

'Perhaps we'd better go,' said George, and Daisy said, 'Yes, but where to? Where's it all coming from?' and then she said, '*What's that?*'

That was a scrabbling noise at the side of their burrow. George stood in front of Daisy and the cubs and reared up, prepared to fight. He'd learned to fight since coming to The Wild, and had once pulled one of his cubs from the claws of an owl. He was altogether more fierce and confident than the timid, shy creature who had lived at number 5 Bright Street with Jake and Josh. Now something was threatening his family and all he could think was, 'Let them try!'

Suddenly a nose broke through the soft earth of the

burrow and George braced himself. But a moment later, as the ears came through, he recognized his friend, Capper Fieldmouse.

'Capper!' he cried, rushing forward. 'What is it? What's going on?'

He helped to clear the soft rubble around Capper so that he could climb through, then, much to his surprise, Capper turned and hauled two shrews through the gap.

'Capper – what's happening?' he said as the field-mouse collapsed, panting, on the floor of the burrow.

'Can't stay here,' Capper wheezed, barely able to speak. 'Got to run – hide – get out – all of you – now!'

George and Daisy stared at Capper in bewilderment, and all the little hamsters stared too, with round, unblinking eyes. But Capper was their friend. Without his help, when they had first set paw in The Wild, they would surely have been lost. He had taken them into his burrow until they had built their own, and had

shown them how to forage and how to avoid danger, and cats. If he said they had to get out now, after all their hard work, they didn't know what to think. But they were prepared to listen, especially after another series of loud explosions made all the little cubs whimper. Capper didn't look fit to go anywhere just yet, however, and the two shrews looked nearly dead from fright. Daisy stepped forward and stroked Capper's pelt maternally, wiping some of the dirt from it.

'Capper dear, tell us what's happened,' she said.

Still panting, Capper gasped out his tale. George, Daisy and all the little cubs listened in horror as he told them about being captured and dangled over the mouth of a large, unpleasant human boy.

'Ooh, Capper,' said Daisy, shuddering, and the shrews' eyes were round with horror.

'And it's those same boys who are doing the damage now,' Capper said. 'Trying to blast open the earth with their foolish games. I tell you, I always knew humans were daft – messy and noisy and thoughtless – but this is a new breed, if you ask me – mad and mean.'

Everyone cowered as once more the earth shook around them.

'Well – we can't stay here,' George said. 'First things first – Daisy – take the cubs into the extension.'

'Extension? What extension?' said Capper, and Daisy said, 'But Georgie – where are *you* going?'

'Never mind that now,' said George, and he began ushering everyone out through a tunnel at the back of the burrow. It went steeply downhill, down, down, finally opening up into a much larger space, supported in the middle by what seemed to be a central column.

'We needed more room, you see,' George said to the astonished Capper. 'So when all the fires started up above, we thought we'd dig downwards instead of to the side.'

Capper turned this way and that, hardly able to believe what he was seeing. 'It's amazin',' he said.

'Well, it was all Georgie's idea,' said Daisy, and George went pink.

Actually, though he hadn't said so at the time, he had taken the idea from the Room Beneath the first house in Bright Street, where they'd had their terrible adventure last summer. But also, through living with humans he'd seen how you could design a room much bigger than you needed, so long as you gave it proper support. So George and Daisy and the little cubs had simply scooped out earth around what became a central pillar, and at the back of the big room they were starting the process again.

'There's no limit, really, to how far you can go,' George said, and Daisy beamed at him fondly. 'And it's much safer down here, of course.' From where they were they could hardly hear the muffled bangs and cries.

Capper and the little shrews sat back. They had never seen anything like it.

'And we're still building,' George said, pointing to the back. 'So you'll all have plenty to do while me and Capper set off.'

'Set off where?' Daisy cried.

'Daisy,' said George firmly, 'we can't leave all the little creatures up there to be burned alive. We've got to bring them here.'

'Georgie — no!' said Daisy.

All the little cubs cried, 'Don't go, Daddy!'

'I've got to go,' said George, looking at Daisy, and she could see that he meant it. 'I'll be back,' he said, ruffling the cubs' pelts, 'and what I need you to do is to keep digging. Make this chamber even bigger for when I get back. We're going to need all the room we can get. The shrews'll help, won't you, lads?'

The little shrews nodded solemnly. The cubs clung to George, saying things like, 'We'll do it, Dad,' and 'Don't worry!' but Daisy stood apart.

George reached over and nuzzled her. 'I have to go,' he said.

'I know you do,' she said quietly. 'Just make sure you come back, that's all.'

George smiled and kissed her, then he looked at Capper. 'Ready?' he said.

7 Escape

Frank drummed his paws against the large stone. 'Let me out, you mad rodent!' he yelled, but there was no response, apart from the eerie humming of the hamsters which, if anything, had increased in volume as the night passed. Eventually Frank gave up. He walked all round the ziggurat, looking for a possible way of escape, but there didn't seem to be one. Besides, he was surrounded, on all sides, by mad, humming hamsters. Eventually he sat down again, on the Seat of Seeing, partly to see if it would work once more, partly to see, if possible, *how* it worked.

Nothing happened.

'Well, I'm in a right mess now,' Frank muttered to himself. He stared at the structure around him and he couldn't help but admire the ingenuity, the imagination and the sheer hard work that had gone into it. It was a work as unlike a hamster burrow as anything could be – and it wasn't like any cage he had ever seen either. He stared upwards to where, instead of a roof, all the walls met in a point. Humphrey was certainly clever, he thought, but was he mad?

Frank began to piece together what Humphrey had

told him. He had said that there was some kind of power, or force, running through lines in the ground, and that the big machine, on which the ziggurat stood, somehow generated that force – that was why they worshipped it. Well, Frank had felt the force for himself, that part was true; but what about the New Narkiz, as Humphrey called it, the new land where they would all live, once Frank had summoned the Black Hamster?

But how had he known, Frank thought. How had he known Frank *could* contact the Black Hamster?

Frank thought hard. He could only think that rumours must have spread from the pet shop, since his last adventure. He certainly didn't go around telling other hamsters that he'd met the Black Hamster, they were all too afraid of him to be told. But Mabel did. Mabel mentioned it whenever she could, in order to put other hamsters off Frank. Mabel had said something when he'd first tried to rescue them all from the clutches of Vince, and the hamsters who had returned to the pet shop must have told the others. And now look what had happened.

'*Mabel!*' Frank thought, but he couldn't waste time getting cross now. He needed to think.

Humphrey thought they could use the power in the big machine to summon the Black Hamster – though, in fact, whenever Frank had met him before, he had simply appeared, without any summoning or any mysterious Force. And what if Frank did lead him here and it was somehow all a trap? Frank shut his eyes, thinking hard, and suddenly he knew that the real problem was that he didn't trust Humphrey. He couldn't fault his logic, he seemed to want the same things that Frank wanted, but Frank's instincts were telling him not to believe a word he said.

'So now what?' he wondered aloud.

'A good question,' said a voice right next to him. Frank jumped so violently he nearly fell off the Seat of Seeing. There, sitting at his right-hand side, was the Black Hamster of Narkiz.

Frank stared. 'You!' he breathed at last. 'You – you –' It was all he could say for a moment. Then he remembered all the things he had previously seen. 'Are you – a –' he stuttered.

'An illusion? What do you think?' said the Black Hamster. Frank stared at him some more, then tentatively put out a paw and touched the warm, velvety pelt. It was just as he remembered it, soft and thick, with the sense of some vast, living energy beneath. The ruby eyes glowed into his and gradually a beam of pure joy broke over Frank's face.

He tugged at the pelt, just to make sure, and the Black Hamster put back his head and laughed, and Frank couldn't help laughing too. Then he said, 'You came back – at last! I thought you would never come.'

'I never left you, Frank,' the Black Hamster said.

Frank had so many questions he wanted to ask, but somehow, when the Black Hamster was there, they disappeared. It wasn't that he forgot them, it was more as though, just by being there, the Black Hamster answered them all. Frank started to tell him, gabbling a little, about everything that had happened with

Humphrey, but he stopped when the Black Hamster looked at him quizzically, and Frank realized that he already knew.

'He wanted me to summon you,' Frank trailed off.

'And now I'm here,' said the Black Hamster. 'What shall we do next?'

For a moment they sat companionably, swinging their legs over the mound. Frank felt that he didn't want anything, anything at all except to be here with the Black Hamster, but then he thought about Humphrey again. Should he take the Black Hamster to him – if only to make him realize that he didn't know what he was dealing with, or should they both escape? As he pondered, he realized that there was something he wanted, more than anything else.

'I want to see Narkiz,' he said.

The Black Hamster rose, pulling Frank to his feet. At once, Frank saw before him a desert plain, and strange rock formations he had seen before, leading to the opening that was the Portal of Narkiz. Frank wanted to run towards it. He wanted it so much he was actually quivering, but the Black Hamster seemed to be holding him back. Then the Portal, with its graven hamsters on either side, grew in size, and suddenly they were passing through it, into the great hall with its statues and colonnades, and burrows branching in all directions through the rock. Once again he had the feeling of vast, deserted spaces, the statues crumbling into dust. He looked at the Black Hamster at his side, and the Black Hamster regarded him gravely.

'Show me it as it was,' Frank begged, and at once the great hall was swarming with hamsters, burrowing, chiselling, feeding their young. A hamster passed close enough for Frank to touch him, yet none of them looked at him, or seemed aware of his presence. Another hamster passed and Frank reached out his paw, but he slipped by too quickly, then suddenly he was looking into the face of an older female. It was a beautiful face, a deep golden brown, creased and lined with age, and it was looking at Frank, not through him.

'This is Qita,' said the Black Hamster, and Qita bowed.

'You are of my bloodline,' she said, smiling. 'It is an honour to meet you.'

Frank gazed at her and his heartbeat quickened. His bloodline? Was it possible that she was his great-great ancestress? He looked from her to the Black Hamster, then back again. It seemed to him that there was something similar in their faces.

'You can see me,' he whispered, and Qita bowed again.

Frank looked around. 'These others –'

'They can't see you, Frank,' the Black Hamster said.

'They have the Consciousness of Time,' Qita said. 'We are in the Consciousness that is outside Time.'

Frank had no idea what that meant, yet he felt that he understood her completely.

'Do you – *live* here?' he said.

'In this moment I live here,' she said. 'But this moment is outside Time. I am here to answer your questions about Narkiz. If you will come with me, I will be your guide.'

The next few moments passed like an eternity, or like no time at all. Frank followed Qita through a Great Chamber, to the far end where the Council of Elders met. A group of hamsters had gathered, male and female, and one or two acknowledged Frank as he passed, while others seemed not to see him. Frank couldn't help noticing that all the hamsters were of the same deep golden brown colour as Qita, a little darker than Frank himself, and this, more than anything, suggested to Frank that these were hamsters who had never been bred by humans.

'Wild hamsters!' he thought, and his heart sang with happiness; and, looking at him over her shoulder, Qita smiled. Tunnels and burrows in the rock led away from the Great Chamber, and Frank longed to explore them all; but instead he followed Qita to a high platform and, looking up, Frank saw an opening in the rock and through it the circling stars. He understood from Qita that, while hamsters lived below ground or in tunnels in the rock, they still felt, as birds do, the energy of stars, using them to navigate and to organize their lives.

Of the hamsters they passed, some smilingly acknowledged them, and others seemed entirely unaware.

'How is it he can see me?' he asked, nodding at an elderly hamster who was talking to a younger one. 'And *he* can't?'

Qita looked at him strangely. 'How is it you can see me?' she asked, and Frank had no answer to this. It

occurred to him that whenever he asked a question, it was answered by another one, but he couldn't help himself.

'You said I was of your bloodline,' he said. 'What do you mean? Do you –' he paused and licked his lips. 'Do you know Leila?' he asked.

Qita just looked at him, and he understood that she did know Leila.

'Where is she?' he asked. 'Can I see her?'

'You will see Leila,' Qita answered, 'when the time comes.'

Frank followed her down a series of steps, back to the Great Chamber, where the Black Hamster was waiting for them.

'But I want to see her now,' he said. 'Why can't I?'

'Frank,' said the Black Hamster, 'it's time to go.'

'No,' said Frank. 'I don't want to. I want to stay here.'

'Where is here?' said the Black Hamster, and all at once it seemed to Frank that he was looking, as he had looked before, at the ruins of Narkiz, the desolation of a desert city without hamsters.

'Bring it back!' he cried. 'I want to stay! This is my home!'

But even as he said this, the desert disappeared just as if someone had rolled it up, and he was once again in the ziggurat, on the Seat of Seeing, with the Black Hamster by his side.

'Why do you always bring me back?' he cried, quite petulantly. 'Why can't I live there?'

'You have a place here, Frank,' said the Black Hamster, and just as Frank started to complain the Black Hamster cut him off. 'Frank,' he said, 'your place is in Time, not outside it. You are living Now. And you have work to do.'

'What work?' Frank said sulkily. 'You never tell me what it is that I'm supposed to do. And anyway – what *can* I do when I'm stuck in here?' And he kicked his feet against the Seat of Seeing.

'Well, we could always leave,' said the Black Hamster, and he rose and went to the doorway. 'Unless you'd rather stay.'

'No, of course I'd rather not stay,' Frank muttered

crossly, getting up. 'But how am I supposed to leave, when there's a whacking great boulder rolled across the door. I – Oh!'

For the Black Hamster had rolled the stone away easily.

'After you,' he said.

'But what about all the others?' Frank said in a hushed voice. 'Humphrey and the Knights of Urr? How are we going to get past them?'

'Look around you, Frank,' said the Black Hamster, and warily Frank peeped around the door. An astonishing sight met his eyes. Humphrey stood like a statue with his paws raised, Ivor crouched before him absolutely still, and there were the three big hamsters and all the other worshippers of the Force, unmoving, as if turned to stone.

Frank stared at them, then he turned and stared at the Black Hamster. 'What have you done to them?' he whispered.

'Nothing,' said the Black Hamster. 'But they are in Time, and we, at this moment, are outside it.'

Frank clung to the doorway, hardly able to believe his eyes.

'Shall we go now?' said the Black Hamster and, as Frank stepped away from the doorway, he rolled the stone back into place. Frank smiled as he realized how confused the hamsters would be when they found out he had gone.

The Black Hamster went ahead of Frank, weaving his way among the motionless hamsters, and with powerful, easy movements began to descend the great machine. It was an eerie feeling, passing so many frozen, staring hamsters, some with mouths open, caught in mid-hum. If he touched them, would they feel anything? He brushed past one or two and his pelt lifted again as though with static. Frank couldn't help wondering what would happen if he pushed one of them, and he tried pushing at a small brown-and-white hamster near the edge of the generator, but the hamster didn't move and Frank felt, not fur and flesh, but a dense electric charge. It was as though what he could see wasn't hamsters at all, but points of energy in hamster form. He couldn't move them or speak to them or attract their attention in any way, and this was because they were in Time, the Black Hamster had said, and he wasn't. That was it, Frank thought. That was what he had to ask about, before the Black Hamster disappeared from him again, and he chased him as hard as he could, but he soon found that it was all he could do to keep up.

Out of the big chamber that contained the great machine the Black Hamster went, entering the pipeline which Humphrey had led Frank along before, and he travelled along it now faster and faster, with Frank scrambling furiously behind, until all thought of questions had gone from him and he just ran as fast as he could without pausing, even for breath. And as he ran he noticed that the humming noise, and the Static Charge, had entirely disappeared, as though that too was frozen in mid-flow.

The pipeline opened out into the small box-like room that Humphrey had called the Shrine of the

Holy Junction. They went past the first and the second, and at last, in the third junction box, the Black Hamster paused. He was apparently untroubled by the long run, and Frank also found, much to his surprise, that he wasn't out of breath either. In fact, if anything, he felt invigorated.

The Black Hamster looked at him, smiling. 'From here you can get back to the houses,' he said.

'Oh,' said Frank. Then he said, 'I don't want to go back to the houses.'

The Black Hamster looked at him.

'Why can't I stay with you?' Frank said.

The Black Hamster said nothing.

'You never answer my questions,' Frank said. 'There's so much I want to know – about Narkiz – and – all this business about being in and outside time – what's that all about? And why do you keep disappearing? Why don't you show yourself to the other hamsters – I mean – why me?'

The Black Hamster went on looking at Frank, but it was as though he was also looking at a vast stretch of time, past and future, that went on without end.

'Not everything can be explained,' he said, and Frank knew that it was true, there were some things that you have to find out for yourself.

'But why do I have to keep going back?' he said. 'Can't I stay with you?'

'You have a place here,' the Black Hamster said.

'In a *cage*,' Frank said hotly. 'I don't belong in a cage.'

'You have a place in time,' said the Black Hamster. 'For now you live here, in time. This is where you can help other hamsters who are also in your own time.'

Frank felt that he was grappling with something he couldn't quite hold.

'Help comes from outside time,' said the Black Hamster, 'but it can only work through you, and others who are in time. I work through you, because you are able to help others.'

'But suppose I don't want to help,' said Frank. 'And some of the others – they don't want to be helped. And how am I supposed to help them?'

'You don't want to help?' said the Black Hamster.

'Not necessarily,' said Frank, shifting a little from one paw to the other. 'I'd rather stay with you.'

'You would rather stay with me,' said the Black Hamster, 'and not help?'

Frank looked at the Black Hamster. He could see himself reflected in each of the ruby eyes. He had been about to say, 'Yes, that's right,' but the words died on his lips. The Black Hamster worked to help all hamsters, he could see that, and if he had to work through some hamsters, those who were receptive to his Call, then that was the way it was.

Yet still Frank was reluctant to give up. 'Can't I stay with you?' he said carefully. 'Outside time, and work with you to help other hamsters?'

'You have chosen to help,' said the Black Hamster. 'The way of helping is not for you to choose.'

'Then I don't want to help,' said Frank rebelliously. 'Take me back to Narkiz and I'll stay there.'

There was a moment of complete silence.

'I will take you back to Narkiz,' the Black Hamster

said, 'if you tell me again that you do not want to help.'
And he looked at Frank, and the sharp points of his
teeth gleamed.

Frank understood. This was what Mabel had meant,
all that time ago, when she said that the Black Hamster
was a Force that Lured other hamsters to their Doom.
Frank could face that Doom now, here, in this junction
box away from the houses, feel the sharpness of those
teeth, the hot breath on his neck. He felt a qualm of
fear.

'Courage,' said the Black Hamster unexpectedly.
Frank looked at him without flinching, and suddenly
he saw what it would mean to go with the Black
Hamster and turn his back on all other hamsters; to
live in a world without time, while other hamsters
struggled on. Briefly he had a sense of hamsters everywhere, some lonely, some neglected or badly treated, all
of them taken away from their natural home, and all of
them getting on with their lives as best they could.
That was what Courage meant.

'It is a choice you have already taken,' said the Black
Hamster softly.

Frank dashed a tear from his eye.

'But how am I supposed to help?' he said. 'They
don't all want to leave their cages and come with me.
And if they did – where would I take them?'

'You can only help each hamster in the way that he
or she needs,' said the Black Hamster gravely. 'Anything
else is a waste of time.'

Frank dashed away a tear from his other eye. He felt
forlorn.

'They don't need me,' he said.

The Black Hamster sighed. He seemed to feel Frank's troubles as keenly as Frank did himself. 'There is one hamster who needs you very much now,' he said.

Frank gave his eyes a final wipe and ran his paws quickly over his face.

'What do you mean?' he said. 'Where?'

'In the houses,' said the Black Hamster.

Frank thought quickly about the other hamsters in Bright Street. Mabel? Maurice? Not George – he wasn't there any more. Elsie?

Frank looked at the Black Hamster. 'Is it Elsie?' he said.

'You won't find her in the usual place,' the Black Hamster said. 'Follow the scent. And use your instincts. Hurry,' he said, and his voice was fading. For a moment Frank felt torn between the desire to watch him, to try to see where he was going, and the urge to help Elsie; but he hesitated for only a moment before setting off along the line that led from the junction box to the houses. He felt better already, because he had something definite to do. His heartbeat raced again, his breathing quickened and the wire above him began to hum once more. Elsie was in trouble and Frank had to find her, that was all he could think about. All thoughts of abandoning hamsters to their fate were gone.

8 Fire

Elsie, still in the birdcage, had been getting to know Mrs Timms. She was a kindly old woman who shuffled around in her dressing gown with a glass of gin in one hand and a tin opener in the other. Even before breakfast she seemed to have drunk rather a lot of gin, and now she seemed to think that Elsie *was* her budgie, Bobby. She was delighted to find her there when she got up.

'Bobby, you've come back,' she said. 'Just like the old times.' She shuffled over to the cupboard. 'Now, you must eat.'

Elsie was very hungry by this time, and Mrs Timms made them both some toast.

'Now, you won't fly away if I open the door?' she said, and Elsie looked at her mournfully. But the toast was nice and she stuffed some of the larger pieces into her pouches for later.

Mrs Timms beamed through the bars of Elsie's cage. 'Who's a pretty boy then?' she said, several times. 'You are, yes you are. I'll get some lovely birdseed for you. Shoo, kitties!' she said to the cats who had gathered hungrily around the base of the stand. 'You leave my

Bobby alone.'

She fed a large number of cats who seemed to have wandered in from the streets, then she settled in her chair, still talking to Elsie.

'When I first came here, from the old country, with my Cyril,' she said, 'the first thing I said to him was, "We'll get a birdie, Cyril – to remind me of the old days." In Hungary I always had a bird.'

She talked quite a lot to Elsie during the course of the day. She told her about marrying an English soldier after the war and coming to live with him in a street not far away from Bright Street. She said that she used to be a dancer in a bar in Budapest, and that was where she had met him. Hungary suffered terribly in one war after another, and she had lost all her family. She had been lonely at first in England, and they hadn't had any children, but she and Cyril had been devoted to one another. Then Cyril had died, and she had sold the bigger house and come to live in Bright Street. That was years ago, and now the cats were her only company.

'More and more I think about the old country,' she said. She tapped Elsie's cage again. 'You and me, we know what it is like to live in a strange country,' she said. 'We will always be strangers here.'

Elsie knew what she meant, though until that moment she had never given it much thought. She knew suddenly why Frank longed for a place of his own. She had been longing to get back to Lucy's house and her own cage, but now suddenly she felt a deeper loss. Though she had been born in a pet shop, and had never seen the desert, she felt suddenly the call of ancient territory. It was as though she was absorbing Mrs Timms's mood. Whenever she came near the birdcage Elsie felt powerful waves of loss coming from the old woman, almost like a smell, along with the gin and cat wee. And when she talked about the old country her voice changed and her accent thickened.

'Ah, the smell of goulash in the little cafés,' Mrs Timms said. 'And the music – the music would break your heart, and the dancing.' She teetered round the room in a rather wobbly way, then stumbled into her chair and promptly fell asleep. And when she woke up she was delighted, all over again, to see Bobby in his cage.

And so the day passed. There was no pattern to it that Elsie could see. Mrs Timms dozed and woke, and fed the cats from an endless supply of cat food, talking all the time in a rather hoarse but musical voice about picking vegetables in the old country, and the moon rising over fields of maize and hanging there so low you almost thought you could touch it, and the smell of paprika, and fermented milk. She ate little herself, for all her talk of food, and she didn't get dressed, but put the little electric fire on in front of her armchair and dozed frequently. Once she woke suddenly with a start and said, 'Birdseed!' and began at once to pull an old tweed coat on over her nightie.

'Don't worry, Bobby,' she mumbled. 'I'll fetch food,' and she shuffled out in her slippers, tweed coat and nightie, leaving the door wide open.

Elsie ran to the door of her cage and opened it, but it was a long, dizzying way down, and she was too far from either the curtain or the chair to leap out. Mrs Timms had obviously worked out that if she left the birdcage too near the curtains, the cats could climb up them and get at it. As it was, they were prowling round the base again, tails twitching, looking up at Elsie with lemon eyes. So even if she did make a jump for it, she would probably fall straight on to a cat.

Elsie wasn't at all comfortable on her own with all these cats, and Mrs Timms seemed to be gone for ages. The cats mewed and rubbed themselves against the stand. One climbed on the windowsill and another on to the back of the chair, gazing at her. She could hear them talking to one another in their strange language.

'Can't we push it over?' one said, and jumped up against the stand. Elsie's cage rocked, but the stand stood firm.

'Maybe if we all push together,' another suggested, and three of them attacked the stand at once. Elsie's cage rocked more violently this time but, to her vast relief, the stand still held.

'Let me have a try,' said a silky voice. It was Sergeant, from Jackie's house. The other cats cleared a path for him and he prowled round the base, gazing upwards. Then he backed away and crouched, wiggling his hips from side to side. Suddenly he sprang at the stand.

The tall stand crashed towards the window, with Sergeant clinging on to it for dear life. Elsie rolled over and over in her cage as it clanged into the glass and one of the cats gave a yowl of triumph.

But just then Mrs Timms burst into the room and began shooing all the cats away with a brush. 'Bad cats! Bad kitties!' she cried, and for a few moments there was chaos, as cats flew in all directions and Mrs Timms wielded her broom. Elsie's world spun and lurched as Mrs Timms stood the birdcage up again, and the next thing she knew she was gazing up at Mrs Timms's big red nose.

'Bobby, Bobby!' cried Mrs Timms. 'Have they hurt you, Bobby?'

Slowly Elsie got to her feet. Mrs Timms's face, with its mottled cheeks and watery eyes, loomed over her. She felt quite sick and her heart was racing.

'I'm all right,' she managed to say. Mrs Timms opened the door, picked Elsie up and kissed her several times, which was not at all pleasant, owing to the sour smell of alcohol on her breath. She flattened herself into Mrs Timms's cupped palms.

'Never mind, my Bobby,' Mrs Timms said. 'I'm with you now. I won't go away again.' Gently she put Elsie back into her cage. 'I've got something nice for you,' she said, and she poked in a long stick covered in seeds. 'This is from the nice man in the pet shop,' she said, but Elsie felt too shaken up to eat. Besides, it was birdseed.

'I'm not Bobby,' she said to Mrs Timms. 'Look at me – I'm not a budgie!'

Just for a moment the watery eyes seemed to clear.

'Why – you're not my Bobby,' said Mrs Timms wonderingly. 'You – you're a –'

But just then there was a tremendous crash as one of the fleeing cats knocked a jug off the sideboard.

Mrs Timms spun round. 'Naughty Stinker!' she cried. 'Out with you – out! Out! And leave my Bobby alone!'

She chased away the remaining cats, then picked up her knitting, still muttering to herself, and sat down in her armchair.

'Don't you worry, Bobby,' she said. 'You'll be safe now.'

Elsie stared at her in despair. Mrs Timms continued to talk to her as she began to knit, all about the first time she met Cyril.

'I wore a beautiful red silk dress that shimmered like the stars. And he was handsome, like a prince, and we danced and danced, da – da – te – dah.' Mrs Timms, humming, finished one line of the shapeless blue knitting, then another. Then she put the electric fire on and toasted her feet. Her head began to nod slowly forward as she knitted, and soon she was snoring gently. One cat returned, then another, but they ignored Elsie this time and went straight to their food. Outside, dusk gathered and the fireworks began. With each explosion Mrs Timms's head jerked slightly, and she mumbled but didn't wake up. The cats didn't like the explosions any more than Elsie did. Their fur lifted and they yowled. One hid under the table and two others started to fight. They flew round the room, attacking each other and getting tangled in the knitting. Balls of wool scattered, the shapeless blue garment slowly unravelled and still Mrs Timms didn't wake up. Round and round the cats went, banging into the furniture and into Elsie's stand again, which shook but didn't give. The wool became tangled around the legs of chairs and looped around the stand. Finally the two of them ran out, still fighting.

Elsie couldn't believe that she was still trapped in the birdcage. Surely she wouldn't have to spend the rest of her life here? She liked Mrs Timms and did feel sorry for her in a way, but she did wonder why she never got dressed, or groomed herself. Elsie was always grooming herself. And why hadn't she made friends with the other people in Bright Street?

The thought of living out her life in a birdcage in Mrs Timms's front room, with all the cats, caused a tear to drop off the end of Elsie's nose and quiver along the length of her whiskers. 'Lucy will be sad,' she thought.

Loud music drifted along the street from number 1. Sean's father had got out his electric guitar and Sean was on drums. A little later, there was more loud music from number 13 as Guy's friends arrived to rehearse. Elsie couldn't sleep, and anyway there was nowhere to sleep in the cage. Every time someone passed the window her heart leapt, then sank again as they walked by, ignoring the small hamster jumping up and down in a birdcage. Now she gnawed disconsolately at the birdseed, which actually didn't taste too bad. 'I wonder what the others are doing,' she thought. She fretted and became more and more nervous as the noise increased. She still hadn't warned George, she thought, after an extra loud series of sizzling bangs. Whatever would happen to George and Daisy and the cubs?

Suddenly there was a loud sizzling noise from *inside* the room. Elsie jumped in alarm and gazed wildly around. There were no pans on in the kitchen but – there it was again! And now she could definitely smell smoke.

The next thing Elsie knew, there was a burst of flame from the electric fire by Mrs Timms's feet. There was another loud sizzle, another burst of flame, and a small tongue of flame ran along a strand of wool to the carpet, which quickly caught fire. Elsie stared, horrified. The ginger cat that had hidden under the table emerged with its back arched, spitting. 'What's happening?' Elsie cried.

'Fire, you fool,' hissed the cat, and was gone from the room like a ginger streak.

'Fire!' cried Elsie. She had never seen fire at such

close quarters before, but she knew danger when she saw it and it was all around her now. Smoke swirled into monstrous ghostly forms in the room and flames licked at the table legs.

'Mrs Timms – wake up!' Elsie cried, but Mrs Timms's head only sank even further on to her chest. Elsie rattled the bars of her cage. 'Wake up – wake up!' she cried. 'Help me, somebody – anybody – please! Help! Help!'

9 Frank to the Rescue

A tremendous flow of power buzzed along the line above Frank's head. It was so powerful he could feel himself vibrating with it and, yet again, all his fur stood on end. Something unusual was happening, but he didn't dare stop to think about it. He followed the line from the junction box all the way to the houses, and there he did stop. Even from his pipeline he could smell the cats. This wasn't Elsie's house – it was Mrs Timms's.

She is not in the usual place, the Black Hamster had said. He couldn't imagine what she might be doing at Mrs Timms's, but if she was there, with all the cats, then she was definitely in trouble, and Frank had to help.

The pipeline ended in a cable and the cable emerged into Mrs Timms's meter cupboard. From there he would have to cross her front room, despite the cats. And there was another smell, the smell of smoke, that made him want to run away. But it seemed to him that he had been following, like a fragile, silvery thread, the instinct that told him Elsie was here, and now he could detect a faint note of her among all the dreadful smells. 'Courage!' he told himself, and he began to climb up the cable.

Even before he reached the meter cupboard, the smoke was beginning to trouble him, tickling the back of his nose and throat. Something was on fire, maybe the whole house, and Elsie was in there, with all the cats.

This didn't look good.

Never had Frank needed his courage more. All his instincts, like any animal's instincts, were telling him to run in the opposite direction, away from the fire. The conflict was so fierce that he was actually sweating as he squeezed through the opening at the back of the meter cupboard, but he made himself drop from the cable to the meter box, and from there to the floor. He scrabbled around the floor for several moments, disorientated by fumes, unable to find his way out. Unlike the one in Guy's front room, the door to this meter cupboard fitted securely, but at last Frank found the chink where the doors met and, by pushing, made them open a fraction so that he could squeeze his way on to the oilcloth.

Smoke from the rug billowed towards him and stung his eyes, but he headed for the settee and crawled under it as fast as he could, expecting at any moment to feel the teeth and claws of a giant cat on the back of his neck.

At the other end of the settee he peeped out, choking in the dust and fumes. This was where all the smoke was coming from, and somewhere in here, he felt sure, was Elsie. Desperately he gathered his strength and called her name as loudly as he could, 'Elsie!' and to his vast relief there was an answering squeak – 'Frank? Frank!'

Frank scuttled across the oilcloth with its gaudy pattern. It was all he could see, because the smoke was so dense. 'Where are you?' he cried.

'Here – up here,' cried Elsie, waving furiously.

Frank couldn't imagine where she was, and he couldn't see a thing. 'Where?' he said again.

'Frank – I'm in a birdcage!'

'A – what?'

'Near the window – Frank – climb up on something – hurry, please.'

Frank began to climb up the fabric of Mrs Timms's armchair. A pattern of roses was woven into it and there were lots of footholes where the stitching had come loose. He climbed all the way to the top, flinching a little when Mrs Timms moved or snorted in her sleep, and, once he reached the high back, the air was a little clearer. He could just about make out Elsie, swinging in her steel cage near the window.

'Elsie?' he said, a little huskily because the fumes had got to his throat. 'Whatever are you doing up there?'

'Mrs Timms put me here,' said Elsie. 'She thinks I'm her bird! I've been here for ages. There's no way down!'

Frank quickly scanned the room. The birdcage was near the window, but too far away from the curtains for one small hamster to leap to them. And all the furniture had been cleared from around the stand, so that it stood in a small space of its own.

'Don't you think I'd have tried to escape if I could?'

said Elsie, nearly in tears. 'I can open the door –' she swung the little door forward and back. 'But I can't get down. Not unless I jump. And – I'm scared!'

Frank squinted at the ground. It certainly looked a long way off. And the rug beneath the stand was already smouldering. Then he noticed something.

'Elsie,' he said excitedly, 'Look!'

The wool from Mrs Timms's knitting which the two fighting cats had unravelled was looped several times around the stand. From there it ran round the table legs, so that between the table and the birdcage there were three or four strands of wool, pulled taut.

Frank ran quickly from the back of the chair on to the table. He slid down the leg a little way to the first strand of wool and tried it cautiously. It held, even when he swung from it. Placing his hind paws on the lowest strand and clutching the top strand with his forepaws, Frank began inching his way along the wool.

'Elsie – it's safe,' he called. 'You have to jump – catch hold of the wool!'

Elsie peered nervously over the edge of her doorway. She could see hardly anything because of the smoke. 'Oh dear,' she said to herself. 'Oh my word.'

'It's safe, I think,' said Frank, bouncing cautiously on the wool strand. 'I think it'll hold.'

'*Think?*' thought Elsie. She was dizzy and could hardly think at all.

'Elsie!' called Frank. 'You have to jump – now!'

Elsie imagined, with sickening clarity, the sudden plunge through the air. 'I can't!' she cried.

Frank's eyes blurred and smarted as the smoke

wreathed round him.
'You *have* to!' he
shouted.

Elsie extended a paw
over the edge of the cage
doorway, then quickly
snatched it back.

'Oh, I don't know what
to do!' she cried.

Frank craned his neck, trying
to see her. 'You don't have any choice,'
he shouted. 'It's either jump or burn!'

And indeed, as he spoke, fire caught the lower edge
of the curtains and blazed upwards with a hissing
crackle.

'You have to trust me, Elsie,' Frank called. Elsie
closed her eyes. For just one moment she wished that
the cats had finished her off when they had first caught
her. But that was wrong, and foolish. That way she
wouldn't have a chance, and now she did – a chance
that she might still get to George.

'Elsie,' said Frank, and there was a new note of
command in his voice. 'You have to jump – NOW!'

Elsie jumped. For one terrifying moment everything
went black. She hit the strands of wool and bounced
off them, snatching wildly. Then Frank had her, his paw
clutching at her neck where the cat had bitten, and she
felt a smarting pain. She clutched again and found she
had grabbed the lowest strand of wool. She struggled
and kicked, Frank hauled her upwards, and suddenly
there she was, clinging with her forepaws to the top

strand and with her hind paws to the lowest strand.

'Elsie – you did it!' Frank breathed.

Elsie gasped for breath. The smoke was all around them, swirling into her nostrils. 'Frank,' she spluttered. 'I – I can't see!'

Then she realized that her eyes were still closed.

'It's all right Elsie,' said Frank. 'It's all right. You're doing fine. Now we've got to edge along here – to the table. Just follow me – and don't look down.'

Taking tiny steps, the two hamsters inched their way along the strands of wool. Elsie still had her eyes closed. It felt very peculiar, an unfamiliar way of moving. But soon Frank reached the table and he helped Elsie to clamber up on to the smooth wooden surface.

'Well done, Elsie,' he said.

Elsie finally opened her eyes. What she saw made her wish she had kept them closed. Everywhere there was dense smoke and pockets of flame. Both curtains were blazing merrily and the lampshade was on fire. Mrs Timms slept on deeply, her head tilted backwards now and her jaw hanging slackly open.

'Oh – Mrs Timms,' gasped Elsie. 'Oh, what are we going to do?'

'Never mind about that now,' said Frank. 'Follow me.'

Elsie followed Frank to the opposite edge of the table. At this end the smoke was thinner and the part of the room that Elsie could see was not on fire. Frank ran along the edge, sniffing. The table legs were smooth and Frank groped his way down the first bit, then slid down the rest, landing bumpily on the rug. Elsie landed on top of him, and they both rolled to their feet.

'Where are all the cats?' he said.

'They ran off when the fire started,' said Elsie, covering her mouth with her paws. 'Just like them,' she thought.

'Well, that's something, I suppose,' said Frank. 'Listen, Elsie – I think I'd better get you right away from the houses – to The Wild. I know you want to get back home but –'

Elsie shook her head vigorously. 'No!' she said. 'That's where I was going – to see George – but, Frank – we can't just leave the humans here – Mrs Timms – and Lucy – and Guy – we have to warn them!'

Frank shook his head to clear it. Elsie was right, of

course, but he didn't see how they could do it. And his first priority was to get out of the burning room.

'Now look, Elsie,' he said at last. 'I have to get you out of here. If you come with me now, I'll get you to a safe place – and then I'll come back.'

Elsie stared at him. 'But what will you do?' she said.

'I don't know,' said Frank. 'I'll think of something. But you have to come with me now.'

Elsie opened her mouth to protest, then she shut it again. This really wasn't the time to argue. She followed Frank into the meter cupboard and he helped her to climb up the cable and squeeze through the little hole where it joined the wall.

'Follow the cable,' he called after her. 'It'll bring you to a kind of box. Wait for me there – I'll be as quick as I can.'

He heard Elsie's voice saying faintly, 'But Frank –' then he dropped down the cable to the floor and squeezed his way back through the door of the meter cupboard to Mrs Timms's front room.

Even in the time it had taken him to get into the meter cupboard and out again, the fire had spread, and now it was flickering round the base of Mrs Timms's armchair. Frank could hardly breathe for all the smoke. He seemed to be moving in slow motion, almost as if pushing his way through glue or very thick soup. He reached Mrs Timms's feet in the worn-out slippers with the flapping sole, and slowly, slowly, began to climb up her foot towards the ankle, then along her leg and over the rough material of her bedsocks to the flannel nightie. He climbed all the way up the ruffles on her nightie, over the gentle rise and fall of her chest, until he stood beneath the heavy folds of her chin. Then he began to climb over the soft flesh. Up close, the skin was pitted and bumpy, and there was stubble on her chin. The smell was very strong: the smell of unwashed human (which Frank had never quite got used to, despite all his practice with Guy) mingled with the smell of alcohol – which he didn't like at all – old food stains and cats. He held his breath.

'Wake up,' he told her, clawing at her face. 'Wake up.'

The flesh on Mrs Timms's face was greyish and clammy and she was drooling slightly from the corner of her mouth. She was evidently in a very deep sleep, almost a coma. What could Frank do if she didn't wake up? In desperation he crawled right over her open mouth, staggering slightly as she breathed out, and when he reached the purplish, bulbous nose, he bit it, hard.

Mrs Timms moaned and her head lolled to one side so that Frank fell from her face down to her shoulder. He clutched at the lank strands of grey hair falling loosely and tugged at them, then he climbed up them towards her hairy, purple ear.

'Mrs Timms!' he bellowed in a squeak, right into the waxy interior. 'Wake up!'

Nothing. If anything, she seemed to lapse even further into unconsciousness. Frank backed away from her ear and climbed up the fabric of the chair to the top. From here he could tell that he really had no time left. The rugs scattered over the oilcloth were burning, the little shelves were burnt to a cinder and, any moment now, the fire would reach the meter cupboard and Frank would have no way out. He couldn't stay there any longer. One very powerful set of instincts was telling him to get out as fast as he could, while another was saying that he couldn't just leave her there; and for a moment Frank stood on the chair back, poised between conflicting urges. He shut his eyes.

'Tell me what to do!' he cried inwardly, though he didn't clearly know who he was asking. But then he remembered the Black Hamster saying, 'Help comes from outside time,' and he thought, 'Well, help me then. Help me now. Help!'

And slowly Frank became aware that something was happening. It was as if the dimensions of the room were changing. His scalp prickled. He knew that he was no longer in Time.

'Help,' he said again faintly, and he heard a small, pulsating murmur like a low chant, getting louder. He opened his eyes.

The room was full of hamsters – a vast body of hamsters, stretching in all directions as far as the eye could see, yet still somehow, impossibly, in Mrs Timms's front room. He could see them in and through the flames. And they were chanting, 'Wake, Wake, Wake, Wake.'

For the umpteenth time that day the fur on Frank's pelt lifted. He knew he was seeing, as he had seen them before in The Wild, the whole of the hamster clan. All the hamsters who had ever lived in the hundreds of thousands of years since the hamster race began were gathered here now, chanting: 'Wake, Wake, Wake, Wake.'

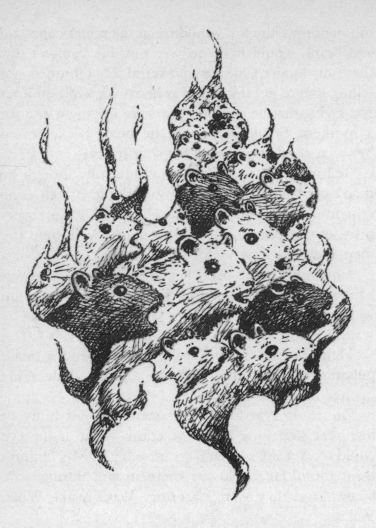

The image he could see was shifting and wavy
through the columns of smoke, but he noticed that
they weren't looking at Mrs Timms or at Frank. When
Frank followed the direction of their gaze, he nearly
leapt out of his skin. For there, in the corner of the
room, and yet seeming to approach them from a great

distance, was a young man, a soldier in army uniform. Over his shoulder was a rifle, but in his hand he carried a single red flower. Nearer and nearer he came. Frank could see a medal gleaming, and the yellow stain of tobacco on his fingernails, yet curiously there was no smell; Frank noticed that at once.

The young man didn't look at Frank, though Frank couldn't stop gazing at him. Was it a ghost? Somehow he didn't seem like a ghost. It was more as though he, in his own time, had come to meet Mrs Timms in hers. Frank quivered as the young soldier stooped over Mrs Timms and, placing the flower on her chest, he kissed her lightly, once, on the forehead. Frank watched speechlessly as two different worlds, two different kinds of time intersected, in a single kiss.

Mrs Timms stirred.

'Cyril,' she said and opened her eyes. The young man smiled down at her, but immediately she was overtaken by a long and horrible fit of coughing, so violent that the whole chair shook and Frank was nearly thrown to the floor. Still coughing, she heaved herself to her feet, spluttering in between the coughs, 'Fire – cats – fire.'

Frank waited long enough to see her stumble to the door and wrench it open, almost setting her nightie on fire. She staggered out on to the street.

'FIRE!' she roared hoarsely, still coughing. 'FIRE! *FIRE!*'

10 Underground

Frank didn't waste any more time. His head still reeling, both from the smoke and from what he had just seen, he scampered down the back of the chair and across what was left of the oilcloth to the meter cupboard. Just in front of the meter cupboard, some newspaper had caught fire. To his left a rug was blazing merrily. There was no way forward. He could try to find another way out, but he had to get to Elsie – she would be waiting for him.

Frank stared at the flames. He had come this far and he couldn't give up now. He had to hope that whatever was helping him would carry on getting him through. He took a deep breath and leapt at the flames. He felt a bump as he landed, then a singeing pain in his tail. But he was through, and he wriggled through the gap in the cupboard door as fast as he could, up the cable and into the pipeline. He was safe. All he had to do now was find Elsie, then somehow they would have to make their way from the junction box into The Wild.

Frank ran swiftly along the pipe, trying to see as he ran whether there were any cracks or gaps through which he and Elsie might burrow into the earth, but the pipeline seemed smooth. He didn't want to take Elsie to the Ark of Urr if he could help it, not while Humphrey and all his followers were there. Besides, he had a feeling that none of these pipelines were safe at the moment. This one was buzzing and humming much louder than it had done before.

At last he could see Elsie's face, peering anxiously along the pipeline from the junction box.

'Oh, Frank,' she breathed. 'Oh, you're safe! I've been so worried.'

Frank climbed into the junction box. There didn't seem to be any gaps or chinks, even where the pipeline joined.

'What happened?' said Elsie. 'Mrs Timms – ?'

'She's safe,' said Frank. 'But we've got to get out of here.' He wriggled round to inspect his tail, which was still painful.

'Oh, you're hurt,' said Elsie. 'Let me see.'

'It's nothing,' said Frank. 'There isn't time. Have you had a look for a way out?'

'There's only the pipeline,' Elsie said. 'We can keep following it –'

'No,' said Frank. 'It isn't safe.'

'I know,' said Elsie. 'It's been making the most horrible noise – I'm so glad you came back – I was starting to think I'd have to go on alone.'

'It's a good job you didn't,' said Frank. If she had carried on following the pipeline, she would have ended up with Humphrey and his gang. He wondered whether or not to explain about Humphrey and the Knights of Urr, but at that moment the earth vibrated, the concrete around them rattled and there was a searing wail.

'What's that?' Elsie cried, clutching Frank.

Even below ground the noise was loud, but suddenly Frank knew what it was.

'Fire engines,' he said, and slowly Elsie released him.

'Oh – well – that's good,' she said lamely.

Elsie's fur was standing on end just like Frank's and they looked like two little hedgehogs. Frank was worried. The air around them was crackling with static and there were little flashes of blue light around the cable.

'Help me find a way out, will you?' he said. He spoke shortly because the pain from his tail was bothering him, but Elsie didn't mind. She thought he was wonderfully brave – returning to a house that was on fire to rescue a sleeping human. She felt almost shy with him now. Together they went round and round the little box but they found nothing, not even the smallest crack or chink where they might start to nibble and dig.

'Now what?' said Frank in despair. He was feeling quite grumpy with pain and worry, and the charged air was giving him a headache.

Elsie looked at him timidly. 'Well – I did notice something,' she said. 'Or I thought I did – I might be wrong – but . . .'

'What?' said Frank crossly.

'Well – a little while ago there was a kind of sizzling noise, and then another – rather like when water falls on a hot pan.'

'Water?' said Frank, and both hamsters peered upwards. There, above the cable, it was just possible to see a long crack in the concrete box, and the ceiling looked dented, almost as if it was caving in.

'Elsie, you're a genius,' said Frank, and Elsie beamed. 'Help me up, will you?' he said.

Taking great care to avoid the cable which was vibrating in an alarming manner, Frank climbed on to Elsie's shoulders. From there he could easily reach the crack and, through it, smell earth. He clawed at it and a little chunk of concrete fell away.

'I think I can get through,' Frank called, scrabbling furiously.

Elsie waited patiently as Frank tunnelled. She didn't move, even when his heels dug into her or when a little shower of earth and stones fell on her. She knew that they were in danger, but she believed, absolutely, that Frank would get them out.

Tunnelling upwards from the little box wasn't easy, but hamsters are good at burrowing, and soon Frank had cleared just enough earth for him to squeeze through. He had to keep on tunnelling so that there was enough room for Elsie, but after a little while he was pleasantly surprised to find that his own tunnel met another that had already been made. The earth beneath The Wild was criss-crossed with tunnels and burrows made by one animal or another, and so it was easy to navigate. It was also rich with intoxicating smells: of earthworms, beetles and moles. Frank felt invigorated now, as though he could go on digging forever, but pretty soon he wriggled round and returned to Elsie, extending his paws through the crack.

'Come on,' he called. 'Jump up!'

Elsie jumped up once and missed, but when she tried again she caught hold of one of Frank's paws. She kicked with her hind paws against the concrete walls of the junction box. He grasped her with his other paw and hauled her through.

'Just take a smell of this!' he said. 'Marvellous!'

Marvellous wasn't the word Elsie would have chosen. *Nasty*, *cold*, *damp* or *dank*, any of those might have done. This was Elsie's first time in The Wild, the first time she had ever felt heavy, crumbling soil on her pelt, or pushed her way through a rough tangle of roots. She felt assaulted by a thousand unfamiliar scents, none of them very appealing to her refined senses. Tiny spiders ran through her whiskers and they twitched convulsively. She was just glad that Frank was there as she followed him obediently through a network of tunnels. However would they find George in all this earth? And what if some other animal found them first? She could only hope that Frank knew where he was going, because she felt totally lost.

Frank went on and on, without showing any signs of fatigue. Soon Elsie began to feel that she couldn't possibly keep up, even though Frank was doing most of the work. She thought sadly of her own little bed.

'I wonder if Lucy's still looking for me,' she wondered, and then she thought that perhaps she wasn't any more, and this saddened her still further. Finally she felt that she had to say something, before she was too overcome with fatigue to speak.

'Frank,' she said timidly, but Frank was burrowing on furiously and couldn't hear. She tried again more loudly, 'Frank – I don't think I can go on much further.'

'What?' said Frank, and he wriggled round, in mid-burrow. His eyes were gleaming and his whiskers twitching. He looked a different hamster.

Elsie looked a different hamster too – a rather sorry-looking, timid one who just wanted to go home. But Frank beamed at her.

'Fantastic isn't it?' he said. 'Just sniff that air.'

Elsie had sniffed quite enough of the air – enough to know that it contained the scents of hundreds of animals she didn't want to meet.

'Frank, I need a rest,' she said.

Frank looked at her and saw how tired and bedraggled she seemed.

'Not much further now,' he said kindly.

'How do you know?' said Elsie.

Frank stared at her, surprised. 'Because of the scent,' he said. 'Can't you smell it?'

Elsie could smell earth, and a lot of different, equally disagreeable smells.

'Which one?' she said slowly. Frank noticed that her eyes had a glassy sheen. He remembered the first time he had come into The Wild, and how nearly overcome he had been by the strangeness of it all.

'The smell of hamster, of course,' he said gently. 'I'm following George's scent now.'

Elsie lifted her head. 'Where?' she whispered.

'Can't you smell it?' said Frank, returning to the trail.
'It gets stronger over here – and just here – and it's
particularly strong just – WOAH!'

'Frank!' cried Elsie in alarm, but all she could hear
was a series of rather bumpy squeaks. Frank himself had
completely disappeared.

Elsie felt a great wave of dread wash over her. She
was all alone in this terrible place. She scrabbled
forward, but there was no sign of Frank. It was as if the
earth itself had swallowed him. Elsie felt almost tearful
in panic. She had known all along that something
dreadful would happen. It didn't do to stray so far from
your own territory, it just didn't do. She called Frank's
name, then lifted a trembling snout and sniffed the air.

There was the horrible jumble of scents again, with only Frank's scent clear and strong. But that didn't tell her much. Except that the scent led downwards.

Trembling all over now, Elsie nosed her way forward, slowly, slowly. She put her paw on to unstable, crumbling earth and quickly withdrew it. This was where Frank had gone – some tunnel had collapsed and taken him with it. For all she knew he could be buried somewhere beneath her. Elsie had never felt more miserable and desolate – not even when George had left for The Wild. She had a choice: either to follow Frank into what might very well be a Pit of Doom, or to stay where she was, alone. She could try to make her own way back, of course, but there was the fire and all the cats. All her options seemed terrible, but she had to do something, and soon.

Elsie's thoughts seemed jumbled into a great tangle inside her head, mixed with the strange scents and noises of The Wild – the scurryings of tiny beetles, the ooze of a worm. She felt close to that state which all wild creatures dread, a kind of paralysis in which it is not possible to think any more. But slowly a tiny spot in her brain cleared. She couldn't leave Frank, he had saved her life. If she stopped now, she would be leaving Frank to his doom, and George too – she couldn't leave George. Elsie's chin trembled and she shut her eyes. She would follow Frank into the Pit, or wherever the steep tunnel led to; all she had to do was to step forward. Her mind went blank as she thought this, and in a funny kind of way that helped, because if she couldn't think of any cheering thoughts, at least she wasn't thinking any frightening ones either. Still keeping her eyes closed, she stepped forward. The earth crumbled beneath her paws and soon she was sliding, then tumbling, further and further down, as though she was falling through the earth itself.

Meanwhile, in Bright Street, the fire raged. Roused by Mrs Timms's cries, the adults woke the children, wrapping them in duvets and blankets, and hurried outside. Tania refused to leave without Mabel, and she spent some time separating the compartment she was in from the rest of her cage, much to the anguish of Mr and Mrs Wheeler. Jackie's hamster, Maurice, was in a simple cage which was much easier to carry, and Sergeant already seemed to have run off, so Jackie ushered the boys out quickly, discouraging them from trying to rescue their PlayStation and Scalextric on the way. Arthur and Jean were already outside because their smoke alarm had gone off, and Jackie banged hard on Guy's front door to wake him up. He eventually emerged, looking crumpled and sleepy. 'Hello,' he said. 'Where's the fire?'

'See for yourself,' said Jackie, hurrying back to Jake and Josh, who were jumping up at the window of the blazing house, trying to see in.

Guy blinked. 'What?' he said, peering along the street. 'Oh no!' And he dashed inside to rescue his guitar, and Frank, before remembering that Frank had left his cage some time before. 'Oh, Frank,' he said. 'I wish I knew where you are.' Sighing, he picked up Frank's cage and joined the others outside. 'What's happened?' he said. 'Has anyone called the fire brigade?'

'I have,' said Arthur. 'They're on their way. As for what's happened – like as not it's one of those kids messing about with fireworks.' He raised his voice slightly for the benefit of Cheryl, Sean and Eric, who were standing outside number 1 and looking as if they thought it was all a bit of a joke.

'HOW DO, MATE,' Eric shouted to Guy. 'NOTHING LIKE A BIT OF A BLAZE TO KEEP YOU WARM ON A COLD NIGHT, EH? BONFIRE NIGHT COME EARLY!'

Arthur bridled at this. 'It's no laughing matter,' he started to say, but at that moment the fire engines arrived with their sirens blaring. Lights went on in other houses on the far side of The Wild, and more people came out in their dressing gowns to see what was going on.

The firemen made everyone stand well back from the houses, and soon quite a crowd had gathered on The Wild, watching the long streams of water from the hosepipes.

'Oh, my poor kitties – Bobby – my poor kitties,' Mrs Timms kept saying.

'Not to worry, love,' said a friendly fireman. 'If there's anything inside, we'll get it out.'

'I wonder what started it?' said Tania's mum.

'ELECTRIC'S ON THE BLINK, I SHOULDN'T WONDER,' Eric bellowed above the noise. 'OR THAT DAFT OLD BIDDY'S LEFT HER CHIP PAN ON. SHE COULD HAVE BURNT US

ALL IN OUR BEDS.'

'Now just hold on a minute,' said Arthur. 'If anyone's caused the fire it's just as likely to be your Sean, messing around with fireworks with those older lads.'

'**WHAT ARE YOU SAYING, GRANDAD?**' Sean's father yelled aggressively. '**ARE YOU ACCUSING MY SON?**'

'Nobody knows what caused the fire,' said Lucy's father, 'so we should probably wait till we find out.'

Eric backed off, muttering, and Angie and Jackie exchanged meaningful glances. Then Angie noticed that Lucy was shivering.

'Are you cold, pet?' she said, putting her arm round Lucy's shoulder. Tears were streaming down Lucy's face. 'What's the matter, love?' her mum asked anxiously. 'You've no need to worry – look – the fire's under control already – it won't spread – your room'll be quite safe.'

'I'm not thinking about that!' Lucy burst out miserably. 'I'm thinking about Elsie! I don't know where she is – she could be trapped under the floorboards!'

Angie didn't know what to say to this. 'Oh no, love,' she said, 'she won't be. Animals know about fire – they know to protect themselves.'

But Lucy wasn't comforted, and Guy, watching her, felt quite tearful himself, because he didn't know where Frank was either. No one knew if they would ever see either hamster again.

Jackie squeezed his arm. 'Cheer up,' she said. 'Frank's a wily little fellah – he's used to looking after himself. He'll be back soon, you'll see.'

But neither Guy nor Lucy felt really comforted.

Soon the blaze died down under the powerful hissing jets from the hosepipes. An area around Mrs Timms's house was cordoned off and the friendly fireman turned to the watching crowd.

'All right, folks,' he said, 'show's over. You can all get back to your nice warm beds.'

Still muttering, the crowd that had gathered gradually dispersed. Jackie, who lived next door to Mrs Timms, went to check with the fireman that it really was safe to return, and Angie led Lucy and Thomas back to number 3. Guy hesitated.

'What about Mrs Timms?' he said. Mrs Timms was sitting on a tuft of grass, wrapped in the blanket Arthur and Jean had provided for her, rocking backwards and forwards and still mumbling about Bobby and her cats.

'THEY'VE GOT PLACES FOR PEOPLE LIKE THAT,' Eric shouted. 'TAKE HER OFF TO AN INSTITUTION AND THROW AWAY THE KEY!'

Arthur glared at him indignantly. 'She can stay with us,' he said. 'We've got a bed in the spare room. And perhaps some people,' he added meaningfully, 'will keep a closer watch on their children from now on.'

'**WATCH IT, GRANDAD!**' Eric yelled, but Arthur and Jean were helping Mrs Timms to her feet.

'We'll all have to be more careful from now on,' Jackie said, holding Jake and Josh by the hand. 'This is a lesson to us all.'

She looked meaningfully at Eric, but Eric and Sean were glowering darkly at Arthur and said nothing. Everyone returned to their homes, hoping, with Jackie, that a valuable lesson had been learned. But the very next day the big boys were out on The Wild again, and Sean was with them. They didn't throw fireworks, but they were still piling up wood into two heaps at opposite ends of The Wild. One of them even climbed over Arthur's back yard wall looking for junk, but he leapt back again when Arthur ran out.

It was the day before Bonfire Night, and the two heaps had now grown very large. Looking out of her window to call Jake and Josh in for tea, Jackie saw that they, and Thomas, were with Sean and one or two of the older boys.

'What are they up to?' she said, peering out.

As far as she could see, it seemed that Sean was handing something out to the younger boys. Jackie leaned forward to get a closer look, and, when she saw what it was, her jaw dropped open. She was out of her house before any of them saw her.

'Go on – give them a try,' Sean was saying. 'It'll be cool.'

He was holding out a packet of cigarettes.

Now Jake, Josh and Thomas could often be naughty, and a bit silly, especially when they were together, but even they knew that it was wrong – and just plain stupid – to smoke just because other children told them to. Thomas backed away and Jake said, 'Nah, it's OK.'

'Go on,' Sean said, 'don't be soft.'

The next minute the packet was dashed out of his hand.

'What do you think you're doing?' Jackie cried. She

stamped on the packet, grinding it into the mud.

Sean stared at her, open-mouthed. 'Eh!' he said. 'That's mine!'

'Do your parents know you smoke?' Jackie asked.

'My dad gave me them,' said Sean with a swagger.

'I don't think so,' said Jackie. She was blazing with anger. 'You should be ashamed of yourself. All of you should!' she added, speaking to all the boys. 'Especially after last night. You're like little kids – playing with matches!'

'Leave it out,' one of the older boys said, and another one said something much more rude, but Jackie wasn't listening. She felt tall and terrible. Sean opened his mouth to say something really cheeky, but changed his mind.

'Thomas, Jake, Josh – come with me,' Jackie said, and she stormed off, pulling Josh along by the hand.

Jake ran after her saying, 'I didn't take one, Mum.'

'I know you didn't,' said Jackie, opening the door of her house. 'I'm proud of you, Jake. But you've got to stay away from those boys from now on – do you hear me?'

Jake, Josh and Thomas all said they would, but Jackie was still really angry.

'Wait there a minute,' she said, and she went round to number 1 and knocked smartly on the door. When no one heard her she knocked again.

Finally Eric opened it, looking bleary and unshaven. 'WHAT'S ALL THE ROW?' he said.

'Your son,' said Jackie, simmering with rage, 'has been trying to give my sons cigarettes.' She glared at Eric.

'WHAT?' said Eric. 'NEVER.'

'I just *saw* him!' said Jackie.

An unpleasant look came over Eric's face. 'I KNOW WHAT THIS IS ABOUT,' he said. 'YOU'RE ALL THE SAME, YOU LOT.'

'What do you mean?'

'STUCK UP, THE LOT OF YOU.' He thrust his chin forward aggressively. 'IF IT'S NOT ONE OF YOU COMPLAINING IT'S ANOTHER – THAT OLD GEEZER AT NUMBER NINE TRYING TO MAKE OUT IT WAS MY SEAN WHO STARTED THE FIRE WHEN EVERYONE KNOWS THAT OLD BAG'S NOT FIT TO LOOK AFTER HERSELF! WELL, I'M NOT HAVING IT – DO YOU HEAR? YOU ALL THINK YOU'RE SO MUCH BETTER THAN US – YOU CAN JUST STAY AWAY – CLEAR OFF!'

And he slammed the door in Jackie's astonished face.

She was furious. She stared at the door, wondering whether to knock on it again and give Eric a piece of her mind, when a blast of music rattled the windows. Eric was playing his electric guitar with the amplifiers on. Angie came to the door.

'What's going on?' she mouthed above the noise.

Jackie told her that Sean had been trying to give Thomas, Jake and Josh cigarettes, that she had complained, and this was the result.

Angie was outraged. 'That's it – I've had enough!' she shouted over the deafening chords. 'I'm going to contact that Mr Marusiak – they can't live here if they're going to make all our lives a misery!'

'Good idea,' said Jackie, and she went back in to the boys, who were playing quietly with the Scalextric.

'What's going on, Mum?' said Jake.

'Don't worry about it,' said Jackie. 'Tea's nearly ready.' But even in number 5 the noise from the guitar was really loud, and through the window she could still see Sean and the big boys messing about with fireworks again. 'I hope Angie does complain,' she thought as she served pizza and salad to the boys. 'But that won't stop the gangs. I bet they're still hanging round even after Bonfire Night.'

She was still cross about the scene with Sean's dad and had quite gone off food herself. But as she left the boys to eat in the kitchen and sat down in the front room with a cup of tea, she had an idea.

'Yes!' she thought. 'Why didn't I think of that before?'

And she picked up her phone.

11 Trapped

All this time Humphrey and the Knights of Urr had been gathered outside the ziggurat, chanting invocations to the Black Hamster. Those in the Outer Circle had been ordered to bring food to those in the Inner Circle so that they could keep up the chant, dropping out one at a time to rest and eat.

The fire at Mrs Timms's set up a great disturbance in the machine, which hummed and buzzed.

'It is nearly time, friends!' cried Humphrey, dancing with excitement. 'Keep it up! Keep it up!'

Then when Eric switched his amplifiers on, the air fairly zinged with static.

'He is coming!' cried Humphrey in transports of joy. 'He is coming!'

The buzzing noise from the great machine altered, shifting tone.

'Now!' cried Humphrey. 'Now is the time! Ivor – open the doors!'

The little crooked hamster scuttled forward at surprising speed. Humphrey put on his red ribbon and stood up very straight. All the hamsters fell silent. Panting and straining, Ivor, with two of the biggest hamsters, rolled back the stone from the doorway and peered round it. Then he went inside and after a moment or two came out again, his eyes glassy with shock.

'Master,' he said. 'It – It is empty!'

A gasp went up from the assembled hamsters.

'What?' said Humphrey. 'Don't be a fool!'

Ivor quailed.

'M–Master can see for himself – if he wants,' he said.

With a quick glance at the surrounding hamsters, who had shuffled forward, craning to see, Humphrey stepped towards the ziggurat. He made the same strange gestures with his paws that he had made before and he mumbled the Words of Power, then he stepped into the ziggurat. There was the Seat of Seeing, the little altar and the mousetrap with the cables, but there was no sign of Frank, or of the Black Hamster. Humphrey walked all round the little temple, sniffing, thinking furiously and playing for time. Then he leaned against one of the stones and closed his eyes. When he reappeared at the entrance, however, he seemed once more in command.

'Fellow Knights,' he said clearly, 'this is a powerful sign that the magic is working.'

The other hamsters looked at one another, then back at Humphrey.

'For it is written,' Humphrey said, his voice now rising rather shrilly, 'that the Chosen One shall ascend to his Master, to the Unmanifest Zones, to bring Him here.'

There was some muttering and shuffling in the

ranks. This was the first they'd heard of it.

'You mean he's gone?'

'But how?'

'I want to see.'

Humphrey raised his paws. 'Whatever we do, we must not interrupt the magic now,' he said. 'The Rites of Power work in their own time. We must carry on with the invocation, or the magic will fail.'

'Not more chanting,' said one hamster.

'How much longer?' said another.

'You said the time was now.'

'This is High Magic,' said Humphrey sternly, 'which has not been practised since the Dawn of Time. It will work – it *is* working – but the energy must be sustained. You can see for yourselves that the Flow of Power has greatly increased – would you throw away all your efforts now?'

'I'm tired,' said a small hamster at the back, and another one said, 'I want to go home.' And one of the biggest hamsters said, 'We can't keep this up much longer, boss. How long will it take?'

'Master, not boss,' Humphrey hissed. He was in fact very worried because he didn't believe his own tale. He was mystified by Frank's disappearance and really would have liked to start a search, but he dared not confess to the others that Frank had escaped, and that he, Humphrey, couldn't explain how. Besides, if there *was* anything magical about Frank's disappearance, then where would he look? And right now, what he had to do was to keep the Order in his command.

'We will chant through this night,' he said, and he lifted his paws again as voices were raised in protest. 'Or the magic will be lost. By the power of this ritual, the Chosen One has been sent to the Supreme Master, and by its power he will return! You must have Faith, or it will never work. If you do not have Faith, you do not deserve the Kingdom! If you go now – all our efforts will be in vain!'

Humphrey had worked himself into a passion; his eyes blazed and his teeth were bared.

There was some more discontented shuffling in the ranks, but no one said anything, or even moved.

Then Ivor said, 'Permit me, Master, to begin the chant again.'

With as much grace as he could muster, Humphrey nodded, and Ivor stepped forward, straightening his little crooked back as far as he was able, puffing out his chest and clearing his throat.

'Ahem!' he said, then, in a surprisingly deep voice, 'Ommm.'

And slowly, unevenly, the other hamsters responded. 'Urrrrrrr.'

Humphrey closed his eyes again. His thoughts were chasing each other round and round. What was he going to do when the chanting stopped? What would the other hamsters do when they saw that the magic hadn't worked? But maybe the magic was working – at any rate *something* had happened inside the ziggurat to make Frank disappear, and somehow Humphrey was going to have to get him back – but how? This was the question that kept returning and flashing like a little beacon in Humphrey's mind. Where was Frank and, more importantly, how could Humphrey get him back?

After what seemed like the longest time of tumbling over and over, Frank finally hit soft earth, and he lay there, winded. There was an immediate bustle around him.

'Hold up there, mate.'

'Are you all right?'

'Not broken anything, have you?'

'Fetch Capper, quick!'

An assortment of powerful scents filled Frank's nostrils. He opened his eyes, then immediately wished he hadn't, as everything he could see was revolving slowly around him, and what seemed like a million faces were peering anxiously into his.

'Wh-where —' he said, then, 'What —'

'You just lie there, mate,' someone said. 'Capper's on his way.'

This made no sense to Frank, but he did as he was told, since, for the moment at any rate, he wasn't entirely sure that his legs would support him if he tried to get up. Slowly his vision settled, but he still didn't understand. He was surrounded by a cluster of mice, shrews, voles and even a rat.

'Must've fell a long way,' the rat observed.

'It's a long way down,' a shrew agreed.

'Here's Capper now,' said another shrew, and the cluster of faces parted, and another face came into view, a face that tugged at Frank's memory.

'Why – it's Frank,' said Capper.

Slowly Frank's memory returned. He remembered the first time he had been into The Wild, taken there by the Black Hamster to see the wild, dancing hamsters of Syria, who had suddenly all disappeared, leaving Frank alone on strange and dangerous territory where he had rapidly become lost and disorientated. Then a friendly fieldmouse had shown him how to get back to the houses, and that fieldmouse was Capper. He was grinning at Frank in delight as Frank struggled to get up.

'Capper?' he said. 'How – ?'

But Frank never finished his sentence because, with a rushing tumble, Elsie landed on top of him, driving the breath out of him again.

She lay on top of Frank for a moment, gazing in bewilderment at the crowd of faces clustering around. 'Am I – dead?' she said. 'Wh-where am I?'

'You're – on – top – of – me,' Frank said, heaving her off with some difficulty.

Capper helped her up. 'Are there any more of you?' he said.

'No,' Frank said, getting up properly this time. He gazed around. 'What *is* this place?'

'Refuge,' said Capper. 'Good, innit?'

Elsie clutched Frank and stared around in a dazed kind of way. It was an astonishing sight. It was like a very large burrow, with other burrows leading off it, but what was truly strange was that it was filled with all kinds of creatures: voles and rats and shrews and mice – there was even a mole, a hedgehog and some rabbits. Above them a tangle of roots made the ceiling, and to one side there were thick columns of earth. At the far end the walls seemed to have collapsed into rubble.

'Any animal that needs help can come here,' said Capper solemnly. 'But we're still building it, as you can see. I'll explain it all in a mo, but for now you could probably do with some food. Miska, Lattie, bring our guests some eatables.'

Two little voles ran off. Frank was still staring, open-mouthed, at the underground construction before him, marvelling at its dimensions and the skill with which the rough-hewn pillars had been made – when Elsie clutched him even harder and pointed.

'G-George,' she said.

To the left of the great hall the crowd of animals parted, and there indeed was George, hurrying towards them and beaming all over his face. Behind him came Daisy, then Donal, Declan, Danny, Dermot, little Elsie and Dean.

'Oh, it's George,' said Capper. 'He'll explain it all – he was the one who dreamed it all up in the first place.'

Frank blinked. '*George?*' he said. But Elsie had let go of Frank with a cry of joy and was already running towards George, and he to her, while all the little hamsters shouted, 'Aunty Elsie! Aunty Elsie!'

'Looks like food's arrived,' said Capper, beaming, as a small heap of leaves and dead bugs was deposited at Frank's feet. 'Tuck in!'

But Frank was too overwhelmed to tuck in. He

looked at the small tangle of happy hamsters that was George, Elsie, Daisy and all the cubs, then he looked at Capper.

'Excuse me,' he said, and he made his way over to Elsie and George. Elsie was hugging all the cubs, and saying, 'My, how you've grown!' She seemed to have forgotten that she didn't like Daisy, and, although Daisy hung back a bit, Elsie hugged and kissed her as well. Then, as Frank approached, Daisy hurried to greet him.

'Good to see you, Frank,' she said. 'What do you think of our new digs then?' and George pulled himself away from the cluster of cubs and grabbed Frank's paw and pumped it up and down vigorously.

'Marvellous to see you!' he kept saying. 'Marvellous!'

What a lot they all had to say to one another! And

for much of the time everyone was talking at once. Capper ordered more food, and they all sat down at one end of the huge hall between two of the pillars, and ate and drank with the shrews and mice and rabbits and other creatures, and everyone asked questions and wanted to hear Frank and Elsie's story over and over again. Elsie told everyone about setting off to find George and being captured by cats (there were 'Ooh's and 'Ahh's from the audience). She showed them all the bite-mark on her neck, and Frank was impressed because he hadn't heard that bit. Then she told them all about Mrs Timms and made them all laugh about being kept in a birdcage, and finally she told them about the fire, and about how brave Frank had been.

'We wouldn't be here now, if it wasn't for Frank,' she said, and her eyes shone.

George shook Frank vigorously by the paw again. 'Anything I can do for you, Frank,' he said gruffly, 'anything at all – just ask.'

Then it was Frank's turn to tell them about the strange visit of Humphrey, and how he had taken Frank to the chamber which he called an Ark, and how there were dozens of other hamsters there who called themselves the Knights of Urr and who worshipped the flow of energy from the buzzing machine.

'That'll be the substation,' Capper said.

'Substation?' said Frank.

'Where the electricity for the houses comes from. It travels along pipes, like water. I should know – I use the pipes in winter when I'm crossing The Wild – they're always warm.'

Frank looked at him 'So – when the buzzing noise changes –'

'That depends on who's using the electricity,' Capper said. 'Sometimes it's really loud – that's when they're all watching that little box thingy that humans sit round at night –'

'Television –'

'Yeah, right – or when they're heating things up. Then, when they're all asleep, it's really quiet.'

Understanding dawned in Frank's mind. He saw how the hamsters in the substation got really excited every time the flow changed, and probably all that was happening was that the humans were making tea during the adverts.

'What do you mean: worship the flow?' George asked.

Frank took a deep breath. He told them how the hamsters had built a strange temple called a ziggurat on top of the big machine and that they all stood round it, chanting, and everyone laughed. He did a passable imitation of Humphrey mumbling strange words outside the ziggurat, and everyone laughed even more. Then he told them that Humphrey had trapped him inside it, but somehow he didn't want to tell them about the Black Hamster just yet. After all, there were all kinds of creatures here, and most of them had probably never even heard of the Black Hamster.

'So I – er, well – escaped – and I made my way back to the houses – which was when I noticed the fire,' he finished, rather lamely.

'But why did they want to keep you prisoner?' George asked, and the mole said, 'And *how* did you get away?'

Frank shrugged. 'Well – I suppose they wanted me to join them,' he said, a bit awkwardly. 'And I didn't want to.'

'Sounds a bit batty to me,' said Capper.

Daisy said, 'This Humphrey character sounds dangerous,' and Frank knew she was right. But he didn't want to go on talking about it with everyone there.

'Enough about me,' he said. 'What about you? And this amazing place! Tell me all about it!'

George looked as if he still had questions to ask, but Elsie said, 'Yes tell us, tell us!' and Daisy said, 'You tell them, George,' so he took a deep breath and began.

'Well,' he said, 'we needed an extension for the cubs – so we dug downwards because of the roots above. Then those louts started pushing their fireworks into the earth – into the holes the animals here created for coming and going across The Wild. Some lost their homes, others their lives.'

'Our burrow just collapsed,' a mournful-looking rabbit put in.

'And ours blew into the air,' squeaked a shrew.

'It was chaos,' said Capper. 'Animals running for their lives, or trapped in their own burrows – the rescue work's still going on.'

'I came across Capper leading two injured shrews to safety,' said George. 'And I knew we couldn't just leave them – especially when it was Capper who showed us around when we first came to The Wild. So me and

Daisy took them to the new extension – it was deep enough, you see, to be safe from the blasts. But when Capper told us how many animals were in danger, we thought – well – we'd better keep digging. And that's how it started.'

'Any animal can come here who needs to,' said Daisy. 'But they've all got to dig. It's too big a job for a couple of hamsters.'

'We don't mind digging,' said a vole, 'if it means we can keep our families safe.'

'And when it comes to finding food,' said a rat, 'we all chip in – them as can dig do, and the rest of us find food. Digging's hungry work.'

Frank still looked bewildered. 'You mean you all share the work –' he began.

'Of staying alive,' Capper finished triumphantly, grinning. 'It's a new one, I know – but it works!'

It certainly was a new idea. Frank had heard of hamsters working together before, of course – but hamsters, rats, voles, shrews, moles and rabbits? That was certainly new. Most species kept to themselves.

'It's all thanks to George,' said Daisy, and the animals agreed.

George went pink around the nose. 'Oh well,' he said bashfully. 'It seemed sensible, really. I just thought that since we were all in danger, we all had to work together – build a bit here – dig a tunnel there – and the archways just sort of happened – but look – I'll show you – would you like a look around?'

Frank and Elsie certainly did want to look around, though Elsie still felt a bit nervous in the presence of all these other animals; but George held her paw as they set off, and Capper walked with Frank.

'That tunnel that you fell down's new,' he told Frank. 'George said that we needed another entrance, but it had to be steep enough so that if anyone stuffed a firework down it, we'd still be safe. But we're still working on that one,' Capper admitted. 'Looks like it might be a bit *too* steep.'

Together they walked all round the great chamber, admiring the solid pillars and the way in which, at the top, they formed a kind of arch.

'I got the idea from when I lived with the humans,' George said. 'Jackie had the door to the kitchen taken off and the gap made into an arch. And you remember the Room Beneath?'

'How could we forget,' said Elsie, shuddering delicately.

'Well, I know – but that's what gave me the idea of digging down. We can extend indefinitely down here – there's plenty of room.'

Through the archways the tunnels narrowed, and George said that they all ended in burrows, which was where the different animals slept with their families.

'A bit like the houses in Bright Street,' he said, and Capper grinned.

'I never thought any good could come from living with humans,' he said, 'but now look! We can extend across most of The Wild like this. We share food and take decisions in the main chamber, but we've still got our private spaces. And any animal's welcome, provided they work with the rest of us.'

George looked at Elsie. 'Do you like it, Els?' he said.

Elsie's eyes were shining and for a moment she couldn't speak. She was remembering how troubled and timid George had been when she first met him, and now, here he was, a leader of animals, surviving in The Wild.

She squeezed his paw. 'Oh George,' she said, 'I think it's marvellous. Isn't it marvellous, Frank?'

Frank had said hardly anything during the whole tour, but now that they were looking at him he said, 'But what happens when the fireworks are over and done with? Will you all go back to your own burrows?'

'What – and leave this place?' Capper laughed.

George said, 'Some may want to, of course, but it'll be easy to create pathways from the different chambers back to the old burrows, and then they can all come back here when there's any danger. It's a refuge. We work together, we survive together – we don't work together – we're lost.'

George looked so determined and courageous as he said this that Elsie flung her arms round him and kissed his nose.

But Frank was still overwhelmed by conflicting emotions. It was a great achievement, of course, and he was very impressed, but he still felt – well, he didn't quite know what he felt. Too many thoughts were whirling round in his brain. He yawned hugely.

'You need a rest,' George said sympathetically. 'We'll make up a bed in the new chamber.'

Moments later, Frank and Elsie were led to a small burrow in which there were two piles of leaves and grass. Elsie looked at her pile. It wasn't exactly what she was used to, but she soon set about arranging it as she arranged her bed at home, so that it covered her completely and she could tuck herself inside.

'You know, this is really quite comfortable,' she said to Frank, from inside her new bed. Then she got out. 'Isn't it amazing?' she said. 'I'm so proud of George – I can't get over it, I really can't.'

'Hmm,' said Frank. He had nosed his bed into the corner, but otherwise hadn't done much with it.

'You must be thrilled,' Elsie went on. 'It's just what you always wanted, isn't it? Hamsters setting themselves up in The Wild – living without humans! Wild and courageous and free – that's what you always said, isn't it?'

'Hmm,' said Frank again. His thoughts were still in a confused jumble and he wanted to think quietly for a bit. He felt, quite unaccountably, sad and alone.

Elsie looked at him curiously. 'And to think it's George who's achieved all this,' she said. 'I'd never have believed it possible – but now I can see what you meant, Frank, I really can.'

Elsie might have carried on in this way for some time, but just then a small troop of fieldmice arrived.

'More food for the guests,' the first fieldmouse said, and they all trooped in, bringing an assortment of berries and leaves, an apple core and some squirming grey grubs.

Elsie thanked them, then sniffed the grubs suspiciously. 'I suppose we'll get used to the food,' she whispered, as the fieldmice left, then she began stuffing the leaves and berries into her pouches. 'Come on, Frank – eat up,' she said. 'Got to keep your strength up in The Wild!'

Frank nibbled thoughtfully on the apple core. He didn't feel at all like talking.

'Are you all right, Frank dear?' Elsie said quietly.

Frank looked at Elsie. She was so pleased and excited to be here – why didn't he feel the same?

'I think I'm just tired,' he said, and Elsie was happy with this explanation.

'Well, of course you are,' she said maternally. 'Who wouldn't be after all you've done? Do you want me to make your bed up for you?'

'No,' said Frank. He just wanted to be left alone, but he didn't want to hurt Elsie's feelings. He looked at her apologetically, and Elsie took the hint.

'I'll just let you get on with it, shall I?' she said and she tucked herself into the pile of leaves and grass. 'Goodnight, Frank.'

'Goodnight,' Frank said. He stared despondently at his bed, then lay down on top of it without any attempt at making it.

As soon as he lay down, Frank realized how utterly exhausted he was. He couldn't sort out one thought from another; they all kept whirling round inside his head. He was almost too exhausted to sleep. His mind ran back over everything that had happened since he'd first left Guy's house: meeting Humphrey, the fire, the ziggurat; and it kept coming back to the Black Hamster and the vision of Narkiz.

All at once Frank realized what his mind had been

telling him all along, what he had resisted knowing – that George's great chamber was not unlike the Great Chamber of Narkiz – smaller, naturally, and much rougher, but essentially the same.

Could it be that what George was building was actually a New Narkiz?

All this time Frank had been hoping to find and restore the old Narkiz. In his secret dreams he had thought of leading hamsters in a march to return to this desert kingdom, even though he knew it was impossibly far away and he had no idea how to get there. Now it seemed that George had taken matters into his own hands. But – a New Narkiz – here – in The Wild? And not just for hamsters either, but for any creature that needed refuge? Wherever Frank had imagined Narkiz, it wasn't here, on his own doorstep, so near the houses of Bright Street. And he hadn't imagined that it would be George who built it.

Frank shook his head. All these thoughts were too big for him here and now, in his present state of exhaustion. He couldn't think about it now, he told himself, he would think about it tomorrow. He closed his eyes.

Strange dreams flitted through Frank's sleep all through that night: dreams of white, chanting hamsters, and ziggurats and fire. Towards morning they all resolved themselves into a single big dream.

Frank was in the desert, travelling towards the ancient city of Narkiz. He felt overwhelmingly happy, as he always did when he returned to what he thought of as his home. On either side of him were desert rocks, piled into towering formations, and as he approached the Portal these rocks became statues of hamsters with noble faces; hamsters who had lived wild, courageous and free. Frank increased his speed until he was running towards the entrance. He had to get there, he had to get into the ancient city that shimmered and glowed in the intense heat as though it was burning.

All at once Frank realized that it actually *was* burning. Flames came from the Portal and engulfed the statues nearest the entrance so that they crumbled and fell. As he drew nearer, Frank could make out the white form of Humphrey chanting before the entrance. He wore his red ribbon round his neck and, as he chanted, more of the statues fell.

'NO!' yelled Frank in his dream, but Humphrey only looked at him, a mocking look, and went on chanting. Frank ran, harder and harder, towards the ancient city, but soon he was surrounded by the rubble from falling statues, and in his heart he felt a terrible despair.

Then suddenly he was far away from the burning of Narkiz, watching with a sore heart from a distant rock, overcome by helplessness in the face of so much loss.

'Lost, all lost,' said a creaking, rustling voice behind him.

Frank wheeled round, and there on a rock, a little higher than Frank himself, was a lizard. Old and gnarled he seemed, mottled in the same colours as the rock itself, and he gazed at Frank with round,

unblinking eyes.

'Creatures come, and go,' he said. 'It has always been so. Change is the Law.'

Very slowly, he blinked, and Frank seemed to see the ages of the world reflected in his gaze.

'We are the Oldest Ones,' he said. 'We have seen. We know.'

Frank found his voice. He waved an anguished paw at the burning city. 'But why is it lost?' he said. 'What's happening?'

The lizard stretched his scaly neck. 'Man is here,' he said simply.

'But can't he be stopped?' cried Frank.

The lizard craned his scaly neck. 'Who will stop

him?' he said, and he craned his neck again. 'Behold, Nations come, and Nations go. But we, the Oldest Ones, survive.'

Frank could hardly bear to look at the terrible eyes in which he seemed to see the extinction of his entire race.

'But it has to be stopped!' he cried. 'Tell me – tell me how we can survive!'

The lizard turned, as if to go. 'Change is the Law,' he said.

'No – wait!' cried Frank. 'Don't go – please!'

The lizard waited.

'It can't be the end of my race,' said Frank. 'It can't be. There are too many of us, surely.'

The lizard said nothing.

'Tell me what to do!' Frank begged. 'Give me some hope – please!'

The lizard regarded Frank silently for a moment. Then he said, 'Man is your enemy and your friend,' and he turned again as if he would go.

'What do you mean?' cried Frank, trying to climb up the rock after him. Something tugged at the back of his mind – something Capper had said. 'Do you mean we have to learn from Man?' he said.

For the first time the lizard seemed angry. He stretched his neck again and his tongue shot out. 'What should the Oldest learn from the Youngest?' he cried. 'Destruction and Chaos? Yet –' he said, more calmly, 'your race is younger, and perhaps able to learn new ways.'

'What new ways?' asked Frank.

The lizard sighed, and it was like the rustling of ancient leaves. 'The old order is destroyed,' he said. 'Yet, if you must learn from Man, then I say this: choose what you learn!'

The lizard's head darted forward towards Frank, over the edge of the rock, then, with astonishing speed and agility, he shot backwards into a tiny crevice, leaving Frank alone.

Frank stared after him in despair. He heard the flapping of great wings and saw vultures circling above, flying towards the ruined city. He saw that the flames from Narkiz had spread and were licking at the base of the rocks on which he stood. Then there was a sudden fall of stones –

'Frank? Wake up – Wake up!'

It was Elsie's voice, piercing his dream. Frank struggled to wake.

'You've had a nightmare, dear,' Elsie said tenderly. 'You kept crying out. And then a bit of the ceiling seems to have fallen –' She looked anxiously round the room.

Frank got slowly to his feet. 'There was a fire,' he said.

'Yes, there was,' said Elsie. 'But that's all over now. You saved us, remember?'

Frank gazed at her blankly. He felt almost as though he was still in his dream. What was he doing here? And where was the lizard?

At that moment they heard George's voice. 'Is everything all right in there?' he said, and his nose appeared in the doorway.

'Oh yes, George,' said Elsie. 'We're fine.'

George came all the way in. 'It's those dreadful boys again, with their fireworks,' he said. 'Looks like they've dislodged a bit of the ceiling.' He went round the small chamber, gazing upwards and tapping on the walls. 'I think it'll be all right,' he said. 'This happens sometimes, but it's nothing we can't put right. You're not hurt, are you?'

Frank and Elsie assured him that they were fine, then they watched as he went round the chamber, pressing some of the rubble back into place.

'Even this far down, we feel some of the effects of a really big blast,' he said. 'We've all got pretty expert at repairs.'

Frank watched George, but in his mind he was going over the dream he'd had. He felt sure that there was some message in it for him, something he had to learn. What the lizard had said was already fading, but what stood out clearly in his mind was the image of Humphrey, chanting before the gates of Narkiz, with that red ribbon round his neck.

'I feel sorry for any creature still up there, near the surface,' George went on. 'I'm going up later with Capper, to see if any more need rescuing.'

All at once Frank knew what it was that he had to do. 'I'm going back,' he said.

Elsie and George stared at him.

'Back where?' said Elsie.

'Not to the houses?' said George.

'No – to the substation,' said Frank. 'There's dozens of hamsters still there – and they have to be told about

Humphrey — he's bad news.'

'But, Frank — it isn't safe,' said Elsie.

'That's why I have to go,' said Frank.

Elsie and George both protested, but Frank stood firm. 'We don't know what could happen with all these explosions,' he said. 'And those hamsters — they've all been tricked. They need to know that there's another way — another place for them. I've got to talk to them at least. If any of them'll come with me, I'll bring them here.'

Elsie started to argue, but George could see that there wasn't any point. 'If that's what you want, Frank,' he said. 'Do you want me to go with you?'

Frank shook his head. 'You've got work to do here,' he said. Secretly he felt that it would be better if he got away for a bit, so that he could think things through.

George looked at him as though he had something more to say, but then he changed his mind. He looked suddenly shy. 'The thing is,' he said, 'we were sort of hoping — Daisy and Capper and me — that you and Elsie would stay — make your home here with the rest of us.'

Frank knew that was what George wanted but, now that it came to it, he just didn't know. But what was the alternative — returning to Guy?

'I'll bring the hamsters back with me,' he said, 'and we'll talk about it then.'

George looked at Elsie, but she looked away. 'Elsie?' he said.

Elsie thought about Lucy. 'I don't know, George,' she

said. 'This is all so strange and new. I will try. I'll stay here until Frank comes back, at least.' She trailed off.

George looked at them both and nodded slowly. 'You don't know where you belong,' he said, and both Frank and Elsie knew it was true. 'Well,' George went on, 'you have to make your own minds up.' Elsie and Frank still said nothing. George said, 'How were you planning to get back to the substation?'

Frank described, as well as he could, the way he had come.

George shook his head. 'Not safe,' he said. 'You'd better come with me, part of the way at least – I'll show you a different route. But we can't set off now – all the gangs are out. Stay and eat with us. Then, when everything's quiet, we'll go.'

He spoke cheerfully, but there was a kind of sadness in his eyes because neither of them seemed to want to stay.

Elsie went up to him and they embraced, and he patted her shoulder. 'I wish you weren't going' she said huskily.

'Don't worry about me,' George said. 'Worry about Frank.'

'I am,' said Elsie, and Frank said she wasn't to, then George took them into the great chamber once more where the digging was still going on and where the scouts were coming and going, looking for new refugees, and they ate, together with Daisy and the cubs. Frank didn't feel too much like eating, but he packed his pouches. He didn't feel like talking either, and he knew that the others had noticed how quiet he was. George was quiet too, and Elsie and Daisy talked all the more to cover the awkward silences.

After supper, some shrews sang to them, then Daisy said, 'Time to put the cubs to bed. Come on, Elsie, you can help me pick the fleas off their pelts if you like.'

'Oh – er – well,' said Elsie, but she could see that Daisy wanted to give George and Frank some space, so she followed Daisy out of the big chamber.

One of the scouts came down to tell them that all was quiet on the heath.

George looked at Frank and made himself smile. 'Ready?' he said.

He led Frank along a narrow little passage that became broader and rougher, more like a tunnel made by wild animals, which in fact it was. They followed this for a while without speaking, then the tunnel began to twist and turn and climb. Finally, when Frank supposed they must be near the surface, it branched, and George paused.

'I'm going this way,' he said. 'That way'll bring you out near the substation.'

Frank clasped George's paw. He wanted to say that he was grateful, and very impressed – he thought it was all wonderful, and he didn't know quite what his problem was – but words failed him and instead he just squeezed George's paw.

George smiled, but Frank knew that he wasn't happy. 'You're on your own now,' he said, and he looked as though there were other things he would like to say, but all he said was, 'Take care,' and then he disappeared into the branching tunnel, leaving Frank to make his own way back to Humphrey and the Knights of Urr.

As Frank drew near the substation, he climbed upwards to the surface of The Wild. Something must have happened, because it wasn't that late, but all the gangs had gone. It was a beautiful, frostbitten night, eerily quiet. Each strand of grass was stiff and sparkling, the earth was hard, and colder than Frank had ever known. Still he wanted to be there, in the tingling cold where the sharp air cleared his thoughts. Snails clung to the undersides of leaves, their trails glistening. Up above him, he knew, were the stars, though he couldn't see them, and all around him the earth hummed with an energy of its own that was quite unlike the buzzing of electricity, but came from the millions of different lives lived on or beneath its surface – the lives of plants and beetles and worms. Frank felt the energy of it through his paws and his nose. All around him, in this one moment, an infinite number of things were happening: tiny creatures coming into life or leaving it, plants breathing through their leaves and putting down roots, and far, far away, stars bursting into life and dying. 'Change is the Law,' he thought, and somehow it helped. If the New Narkiz could not be exactly like the old, then perhaps that was not a bad thing.

Frank peered through the grass and leaves towards the substation. It was just a small, concrete shed. It didn't look impressive at all from the outside. He realized he would have to use the line of power to get in, and he began to burrow again. He found it without too much difficulty, but he had to scrabble up and down it for a while before he found a chink that he could squeeze through. Inside the pipe, the line still seemed very disturbed, as though still affected by the electrical fault in Mrs Timms's house, or by the amplifiers in Eric and Sean's house. The line zinged and hummed, and once more Frank felt all the fur on his pelt lift and his whiskers tingled. He approached the entrance to the substation warily, listening for chanting. Instead what he heard was a great cacophony of hamster voices, raised as though an almighty argument was going on.

In fact, an almighty argument *was* going on. After several hours of chanting, one of the bigger hamsters had suddenly stopped and said, 'I've had enough of this – I'm going home.'

'Who dares to challenge the Power of Urr?' cried Humphrey.

'I do,' said the big hamster with one eye; and another hamster said, 'Me too!' and soon lots of other voices were raised.

'I'm tired!'

'I'm bored!'

'My feet hurt!'

'My throat hurts!'

'Friends!' cried Humphrey, looking round wildly. 'Have you forgotten our common purpose, and Vision? Of a Kingdom of Hamsters, united under the One?'

'Well, where is he then?' said the big hamster, and another voice cried, 'Open the ziggurat!'

And soon everyone was calling out, 'Yes open it!'

'Open the doors!'

'We want to see!'

Now Humphrey had kept them going all this time on the promise that the Chosen One (Frank) would return, bringing with him the Supreme Master, but in fact he wasn't at all certain that this would happen, and he was very much afraid that when he opened the door the ziggurat would still be empty. He looked at the angry crowd anxiously, and he swallowed.

'But friends,' he said weakly, 'it may not be ready. The Chosen One may still be on the higher levels. He —'

'Well — we want to know,' said the big hamster aggressively. 'Where is he? Where's Frank?'

And this call was taken up too, until it became a chant. 'Where is Frank? Where is Frank?'

'Here,' said Frank, dropping down from the entrance to the dusty floor.

A collective gasp went up and the hamsters wheeled round as one.

Humphrey recovered rapidly. 'Here he is!' he cried shrilly. 'The Chosen One returns!'

The hamsters moved swiftly, dropping from the great machine to the floor, and in no time at all Frank was surrounded. He stood his ground and gazed at them levelly.

The biggest hamster pushed his way to the front. 'Well?' he said eagerly. 'Where is he, then?'

'Who?' said Frank.

The biggest hamster blinked. 'The Supreme Master, of course,' he said, and other voices joined in.

'Yes, where is he?'

'Have you brought him with you?'

'He's not invisible, is he?'

The hamsters pressed forward eagerly. Frank could see their pointed teeth and little, gleaming eyes. He could also see Humphrey, peering anxiously over the edge of the great machine. He took a deep breath.

'Listen to me,' he said. 'You've all been tricked. This place isn't what you think it is – it's just a substation, where the electricity for the houses comes from – that's what the humming noise is – not some mysterious force – it's not magic.'

'He lies!' Humphrey shrieked, hopping up and down on his ledge.

'I'm not lying!' said Frank loudly. 'The electricity travels from here along cables to the houses, and when the houses are using a lot, the noise changes –'

'No!' Humphrey shrieked. 'It's the Great Invocation – the great Surge of Power that will bring The One! It is the sign that the Day of the Hamster is nigh!'

'No,' said Frank. 'It's just the end of *Coronation Street*! There's always a surge of power in the adverts.' His head hurt from all the static, and he was finding this difficult to explain.

The hamsters looked from Frank to Humphrey and back again. It was clear that they didn't know who to believe. But it was difficult to let go of their dream, and Frank's explanation was a bit dull.

Then a look of great cunning crossed Humphrey's face. He licked his lips. 'If there is no magic in the Force,' he said slyly, 'then how did the Chosen One manage to escape? You all saw him enter the Ziggurat, yet none of you saw him leave. Why don't you ask him where he was?'

All the hamsters looked back at Frank expectantly. He sighed. This, of course, was the one thing he didn't want to explain, because it would take too long, and because he wasn't sure that he understood it himself.

'Yes, go on,' said the biggest hamster. 'Tell us how you got out – and where you've been.'

'Yes, tell us – tell us,' cried the hamsters, pressing forward.

'Have you been to the higher levels?'

'What was it like?'

'No – yes – I mean no,' said Frank. 'That is – I've been in The Wild – just burrowing like any ordinary hamster –'

'But how did you get out?' asked a female hamster, and suddenly that was what they all wanted to know.

'Was it magic?'

'Did you ascend through the levels?'

'How many levels are there?'

'It doesn't matter how I got out,' Frank said desperately. 'I can't tell you – I –'

'He can't tell you,' said Humphrey, rearing above them all with a look of triumph on his face, 'because he failed in his mission! And he failed in his mission because he was not worthy! The Supreme Master would have nothing to do with him!'

'That's not true at all!' cried Frank hotly. 'He's telling you a pack of lies! Don't be taken in by him!'

Humphrey could not allow his authority to be

challenged any further, and he would not run the risk of being exposed.

'Seize him!' he cried. 'He has betrayed us all!'

'Stand back!' Frank cried. 'Can't you see that he's stringing you along – he only wants power for himself – he's taking you all for fools!'

'Seize him!' Humphrey cried again. 'The One who fails must pay the price – or the Supreme Master will turn his back on us forever!'

A moan of terror ran through the hamsters and they advanced towards Frank.

'Stop listening to him!' he cried desperately. 'Why don't you ask him to prove any of this? Where's your proof?' he shouted, but already he could see that the hamsters' eyes were glazing over. It was almost as though they were hypnotized.

Too late Frank tried to dart back into the pipeline. Several hamsters seized him at once and, before he knew what was happening, he was being passed over their heads. The ones at the back were running to the front and ascending the machine, as Frank was passed up towards them.

Humphrey was beside himself. 'He has insulted the Supreme Master!' he shrieked, and spittle flew from his mouth. 'He must pay the supreme price!'

Frank didn't like the sound of this at all, but there wasn't much he could do about it as he bobbed and lurched about over the heads of the hamster mob, until he was finally deposited unceremoniously in front of the ziggurat, at Humphrey's feet. His head whirled and his arm felt bruised.

'So you thought to challenge my power!' Humphrey hissed unpleasantly in Frank's ear. 'Now you'll find out what happens to usurpers!'

Frank struggled to his feet as Humphrey addressed the other hamsters, who were pressing forward towards the ziggurat, trying to see.

'The Supreme Sacrifice must be made in the Inner Sanctum,' Humphrey said, raising his right paw. 'And only the Knights of the Inner Circle may attend!'

A general cry of 'Awww!' went up from the mob, but Humphrey raised his other paw.

'If we act now, the Supreme Master may yet be appeased!' he told them. 'We must not run the risk of His displeasure. Do you want Him to turn His back on us forever?'

The murmur subsided and a breathless hush took its place.

'Knights of the Inner Order!' Humphrey cried in clear, ringing tones, 'Assemble now!'

The biggest hamsters pressed forward and formed a rough circle outside the ziggurat.

Humphrey donned his red ribbon. 'Draw back the door!' he cried. 'Ivor – prepare the altar!'

'Yes, master,' Ivor lisped, scuttling forward. With the help of a bigger hamster he opened the door, which yawned in front of Frank like the entrance to a tomb. There was a minute's silence and scuffling noises were heard, then there was a flash of blue light, and all the hamsters gasped aloud. Then strong paws seized Frank and he was thrust forward, through the entrance to the ziggurat. He kicked furiously and tried to bite, but he was flung on to the floor in front of the altar and Ivor advanced towards him carrying a metal chain that looked as if it might have come from a child's necklace.

'Bind him,' cried Humphrey, entering the ziggurat, 'and let the Power flow!'

Once again Frank was borne aloft and carried towards the broken mousetrap that Humphrey had said was the altar.

'Stop it!' Frank cried. 'Can't you see that he's mad?'

But Ivor was already wrapping the chain round Frank, securing him to the steel bar of the mousetrap, and Humphrey was muttering incantations over him, his eyes rolled back eerily in his head. Then two big hamsters grabbed the cable and Frank knew what they were going to do. They were going to make him into a living circuit, and run the powerful current though him.

'You're all crazy!' he cried. 'It'll never work!'

'Power, Ivor!' cried Humphrey, and the two cables met above Frank's head, and blue lightning flashed between them, then they were lowered to the bar of the mousetrap where Frank was bound.

'Now may the flow of Power succeed where our incantations did not,' Humphrey intoned. 'Accept our sacrifice, Supreme One, and come to us!'

He stepped back.

'More Power, Ivor!' he shrieked.

12 Victory

By now you must be wondering what had happened to the gangs.

Earlier that day, as soon as the light began to fade, the rival gangs had spilled out of school and headed straight for The Wild. Rumours of a battle had spread, and more and more teenagers joined them.

'Look at this,' said Arthur to Jean. 'It's like Wembley Stadium out there. I'm calling the police.'

'Oh don't, Arthur,' said Jean nervously. 'You know what happened last time.'

Last time, a lot of fireworks, some still sizzling, had been thrown into Arthur and Jean's backyard.

'I'm keeping the kids in,' Angie said to Jackie as she let herself in with bags of shopping. 'Looks like we're in for a real night of it.'

Jackie smiled mysteriously. 'Oh, I don't think we need to worry,' she said, but she wouldn't say any more. She too went indoors and stood at the window with Jake and Josh.

At first there was just a lot of catcalling and abuse from the members of one gang to the other, then they started throwing fireworks. Planks of wood were lit like torches and hurled across the croft. One of the gang, Bexy, had brought his moped and he rode round the other gang, carrying a lighted branch, before throwing it at the bonfire, which began to blaze.

Then they all began chanting. 'We are the champions!'

'Nananana, nananana, hey hey hey, light the fire!'

Soon there was bedlam. Chanting, yelling, explosions. Bricks were thrown, bottles smashed, and some of the grass and shrubs caught fire. Fireworks were rammed into the earth once more, bigger and better ones this time, and this was what had dislodged part of the ceiling of the burrow which woke Frank from his dream. One side caught members of the other gang, pulled their jackets off and set fire to them. Mrs Wheeler pulled her curtains to so that she wouldn't have to watch – she felt one of her sick headaches coming on. But Jackie stayed where she was, by the window.

She saw Guy going out to try to reason with them, but he was met by a hail of abuse.

Jackie opened her window. 'Don't bother with them, Guy,' she shouted. 'Get back in.'

'Eh! He's called Guy!' yelled Spadge. 'Quick – throw him on the bonfire!'

Poor Guy had to sprint back nimbly, followed by a shower of cans, bricks and fireworks.

Then Eric came out and stood on his doorstep with a can of beer in one hand, egging them on. 'COME ON, YOU LOT! GIVE IT ALL YOU'VE GOT! OH

YES!!' he roared, as a whistling rocket from one gang made a direct hit in the centre of the other and yells and shrieks arose from the other side. Then one member of the other side pulled out a large jerrican of petrol. What would have happened next I don't know, but suddenly, above all the noise and chaos, another sound was heard, the whirring sound of many bikes.

'Yes!' said Jackie thankfully from behind her curtain. 'Come on, Mick!'

From all the streets and alleyways surrounding The Wild, bikes appeared. Not just any old bikes, like Bexy's moped. These were *serious* bikes – Thunderbirds, Norton Dragonflies, Harley Davidsons – with serious bikers on them: muscular, tattooed, with helmets like warriors' helmets. At the head of them all was Matchless Mick, on his Matchless 500. His helmet, jacket and tank were decorated with axes and skulls. He waved to Jackie once, then all the bikers revved their engines simultaneously.

It was a thunderous noise. Jake and Josh jumped up and down excitedly on the back of their old settee; Arthur, Jean and Mrs Timms jostled for a view at the window, and even Mrs Wheeler whisked her curtains back, but Eric disappeared indoors. The bikers were circling the croft, and one by one the gang members stopped what they were doing and stared as if they didn't quite know what was going on.

Then the bikers began rounding the gangs up. Round they wheeled in smaller and smaller circles until the teenagers were all huddled together in a frightened group; then, at a signal from Mick, a tremendous warcry went up, a sort of howling and yipping, like the cries of demons.

The teenagers ran. They tried to run in all directions, but the bikers herded them along very skilfully. The boys ran furiously and the bikers just kept pace behind and to either side. Down one street and up another they ran, their howls of fear mingled with the bikers' warcries until all the noise faded into the distance as the gangs were run out of town.

The doors of Bright Street burst open and first the children, then the adults came running out, laughing, shaking one another's hands and jumping up and down. Jackie hugged Angie and kissed Mrs Timms, then, much to Guy's delight, she flung her arms round him and kissed him too.

'I don't think we'll be seeing those troublemakers again,' Angie said. Her husband, Les, had got his bike out too when he had seen all his old mates, and had driven off after Mick.

'No,' said Jackie happily, 'I don't think we will. Come on, kids,' she said. 'Let's get the sparklers out!'

Frank squirmed furiously as he saw the cables descend. Surely they didn't intend to roast him alive? But Ivor and another hamster were busy coiling the wires at the ends of the cable round the metal bars of the mouse-trap, and any moment now the powerful current would flow round the circuit of which Frank was a part.

'You're mad!' he shouted at Humphrey. 'This won't get you anywhere! Kill me and then what?'

'Silence!' snapped Humphrey. 'You are the offering

to The One. Enough Power will be channelled through you to bring Him to us at last! And then – you will have served your purpose.' He raised his paws over Frank and began to hum.

'Now – wait a minute, Boss,' said the biggest hamster. 'You never said nothing before about sacrificing no hamsters.'

'There's a lot he hasn't said,' Frank shouted, still

struggling with his chains. 'All about his plans to rule you all, to begin with. Has he told you how the new kingdom's going to be run?'

'Silence!' Humphrey shrieked again. 'And it's "Master" to you,' he added to the biggest hamster. 'And as for you –' He prodded Frank sharply with his foot. 'I've waited too long for this day to have my plans ruined by a squeaking renegade! This is the day when my power will be established! The hamster race will reign supreme, and I will reign over it! So the best thing you can do,' he said, 'is die quietly. Ivor – the Power!'

In a lightning moment it ran through Frank's mind that Humphrey had always intended to dispose of him, since Frank would always be a threat to his leadership. At the same moment the biggest hamster began to say, 'Now just hang on a minute –' but immediately a surge of electricity charged through the cables. Frank felt a tremendous jarring sensation, and his whole body bucked and went rigid.

Everything went black. But it was not the blackness of death. The Black Hamster towered over Frank, and the voltage that should have passed through him coursed around the Black Hamster's pelt like flashes of blue lightning.

Humphrey fell before him, prostrate and shaking, and the biggest hamster's jaw dropped. 'Cor blimey!' he said.

'WHO ARE YOU THAT PERSECUTE MY PEOPLE?' the Black Hamster demanded, and his voice rumbled like thunder. The next moment he had picked

Frank up, easily snapping the chains that bound him, and set him on his feet. Frank stood, a little shakily. His bones and even his teeth ached from the shock. But he was tremendously, tremulously glad.

The Black Hamster reared and the ziggurat burst apart. There was a cry of dismay from the surrounding hamsters, and several of them flattened themselves and covered their eyes. Then the Black Hamster picked up Humphrey by the scruff of his neck and slung him into the cowering crowd. 'THERE IS YOUR LEADER!' he roared as Humphrey skidded across the surface of the great machine and lay sprawled in a heap. 'FOLLOW HIM WELL – HE WILL LEAD YOU WHERE YOU DESERVE TO BE LED.' He looked round at them all with blazing eyes, seeming genuinely angry for the first time since Frank had known him. 'When have I ever asked you to worship me?' he asked, more quietly. 'To worship is the human way – it is not for hamsters to set up rulers and priests! If you care to find me, you can speak to me in your hearts. Foolish and deluded hamsters!' he cried, looking round at them all as they moaned and wept. 'You have worshipped power, and that will lead you to slavery! If you want to live like slaves, worship like slaves! If you want to be free, you have only to follow your instincts!'

He paused. Frank was thrilled that finally the Black Hamster was speaking to someone other than himself, that he was proving that he was more than a myth or a story to frighten cubs with. Now at last other hamsters would know what he meant. Then the Black Hamster's paw descended on Frank's shoulder and he felt a flow of energy quite unlike the shock he had felt earlier.

'This hamster knows me,' he said, and Frank's heart thrilled with pride. 'If you need a leader other than your own hearts, then follow him. I will always be with him.'

Unexpected tears filled Frank's eyes.

'He will lead you to a new place,' the Black Hamster went on. 'Or, for those of you who prefer a cage, you can return. You are free — remember that!'

Frank looked around to see how the other hamsters were taking this, and then he drew in his breath sharply. The hamsters were frozen, as he had seen them before; only Frank and the Black Hamster were moving. Frank looked up at him in amazement, and the Black Hamster looked down at Frank. He was smaller now, almost the same size as Frank himself.

A hundred questions joggled for first place in Frank's mind, but before he could ask any of them the Black Hamster spoke. 'I have taken them out of time,' he said. 'They will not understand me any other way. They are too busy cowering before me.'

'But —' said Frank

'They hear me,' said the Black Hamster, 'though they will have no memory of what I have said.'

'But they need to remember!' said Frank.

'I have told them what they need to know,' said the Black Hamster, 'and each will respond as he or she is capable. From now on they need to listen to you.'

'To me?' said Frank. 'They won't listen to me!'

'They will when I am gone,' said the Black Hamster.

'Gone?' said Frank. 'Gone where?'

'They need to listen to a hamster like themselves,' said the Black Hamster. 'If I tell them what to do, they will simply worship me and obey.'

'Well – what's wrong with that?' said Frank.

'I do not want them to worship me,' said the Black Hamster sternly. 'Were you not listening?'

Frank was desperately confused. 'I was listening, of course I was,' he said, 'but these hamsters need to be told what to do.'

The Black Hamster shook his head. 'No,' he said. 'They need to choose.'

'Choose what?' Frank said.

'They must be free – to follow you, or to return to their humans,' the Black Hamster said. 'Theirs is no longer the law of the tribe. They have to make their own laws.'

Frank stared at the Black Hamster. For thousands of centuries hamsters had followed their instincts and the laws of their race. But now he seemed to be saying that they no longer lived in The Wild, so the old laws wouldn't work. This was almost too huge a thought to take in, but he saw something else as well. The Black Hamster belonged to the Old Way, to the time when the hamster race had lived in The Wild. Now that hamsters no longer lived in The Wild, he had become a creature of legend. His time was passing. Perhaps it had even passed.

Frank couldn't bring himself to say this. He swallowed and went on staring at the Black Hamster, who looked back at him with glowing, ruby eyes.

'Yes,' those eyes seemed to say to Frank, 'my time

is over.'

Frank started to speak, then stopped and tried again. 'It can't be,' he said.

The Black Hamster touched Frank's shoulder, and once again Frank felt the powerful current of energy. The ruby eyes glowed into his. 'Courage!' they seemed to say. Frank wanted to argue, but so many feelings flooded through him that his thoughts became jumbled.

'But,' he said finally in a small voice, 'what if they don't follow me? And where will I take them?'

The Black Hamster went on looking at Frank, and into Frank's mind came vividly the memory of George, and his underground refuge. At the same time he remembered how out of place he had felt there.

'But I thought I would be taking them to Narkiz!' he said unhappily. 'I wanted to see Narkiz again – I wanted to live there!'

'Narkiz has gone,' said the Black Hamster.

'Won't I ever see it again?'

In the Black Hamster's look there was a peculiar mixture of sadness and encouragement. But all Frank could think about was that he might never see the real Narkiz, the place he felt he had been promised. Whatever George built in The Wild could be nothing compared to the splendour and beauty of ancient Narkiz. Tears rose to his eyes as he looked at the Black Hamster, and he thought he saw tears in the Black Hamster's eyes as well.

'Has it all gone?' he whispered.

The Black Hamster leaned forward and nudged him

with his nose.

'You can help to rebuild it,' he said.

Frank felt a number of complicated feelings: sadness, disappointment, resentment. He felt that he hadn't been part of the construction in The Wild and he wasn't sure that he wanted to be. It wasn't even just for hamsters.

The Black Hamster looked at him and seemed to read his thoughts. 'New ways, Frank,' he whispered.

Then Frank found the words to say what was on his mind. 'You say I can't take them to Narkiz, because it's gone – but I can take them to the new place that George is building – if they'll follow. But I don't feel part of the new place – it's George's – I'm not even sure that I want to live there. So – what do I do exactly? How do I fit in with all this? I'm not a part of it any more.'

The Black Hamster extended a paw and lifted Frank's chin until Frank's nose was level with his own. 'Your gift is Courage,' he said.

And suddenly Frank understood. He saw that without his Courage none of this could have happened. He saw that Courage was his gift, in the sense that he could pass it on to others – and that was what he had done. He had given them Courage. He lifted his head.

'All right,' he said in a low voice that was almost a whisper. Then he looked directly into the Black Hamster's eyes. 'All right,' he said.

The Black Hamster laughed joyously. He seemed glad all over, and Frank was infected by his gladness. He laughed too, and then he noticed that the other hamsters were stirring, and were whispering among themselves.

'What's happening?'

'What's going on?'

'What shall we do?'

Frank looked around, then he glanced back to where the Black Hamster should have been, but he had already gone.

Frank squared his shoulders and took a breath. 'Fellow hamsters,' he said, 'you do not need to stay here any longer. The Order is over.'

The hamsters looked at one another in confusion.

'Those of you who want to return to your humans are free to go.' Frank said. 'Those of you who want to make a new life for yourselves in The Wild can follow me.'

A murmur ran through the gathered hamsters, then the biggest hamster stepped forward.

'What about him?' he said, nodding to where Humphrey lay cowering on the ground.

Frank went over to Humphrey and nudged him with his foot.

Humphrey cringed. 'The Order – the temple –' he moaned. 'Ivor – Ivor – Oh my poor head –'

Frank could see that for the moment he had taken refuge inside his own mind. He spoke to the crowd again. 'Your leader is no longer fit to lead,' he said. 'You must rely on yourselves now. Not far from here there is a place where hamsters can live in safety – a place

built by hamsters, and shrews and fieldmice, as a refuge
– away from humans and other predators. Anyone who
wants to can follow me there, but you have to make up
your own minds – follow your instincts. You are Free
Hamsters!' he said loudly and quite a few hamsters
jumped. 'And that means that no one, ever, can tell you
what to do. Your instincts will tell you how to live your
lives.'

The murmur was louder this time and more
confused. Humphrey went on gabbling and moaning
to himself. 'Whatever will become of us?' he moaned.
'Darkness, sacrilege – Ivor? Ivor!'

The tattered, clumpy, lumpy little hamster called
Ivor hobbled over. He patted Humphrey nervously,
then stroked his pelt, and Humphrey clung to him.

Ivor looked up piteously at Frank. 'What will you
do with my Master?' he quavered.

Frank looked at them sternly. 'You are free to go,' he
said, and another murmur ran through the crowd.
Frank raised his paw. 'But, Ivor, no one is your master
– unless you are determined to be a slave.'

Ivor bowed his head. Humphrey went on clinging
to him and moaning, then the moan turned into a hum
and Humphrey began to rock back and forth. It was a
pitiful sight, but Frank didn't feel pity; he felt tall and
stern. He watched as Ivor guided Humphrey down the
great machine, almost carrying him and hobbling as
hard as he could. The other hamsters drew away from
them as though from something contaminated, but no
one attempted to molest them. There was almost total

silence, broken only by Ivor murmuring, 'Come on now,' and 'Just put your paw down here,' and 'Only a little further,' as though to distract them both from the silence.

Frank didn't speak until Ivor had helped Humphrey into the pipeline that led away from the substation, and then they were gone. 'Now,' he said. 'Who wants to come with me?'

There was another moment of silence, then the biggest hamster stepped forward.

'I will, if you don't mind,' he said, blinking his one eye rapidly. 'I'd like to see this place. My name's Boris, by the way,' he added. 'And this is my girlfriend, Susie.'

A plump grey hamster with tattered ears peeped from behind Boris's shoulder. Then another hamster limped forward on three legs.

'Rodney,' he said, by way of introduction. 'I'd like to come too.'

Suddenly lots of hamsters were pressing forward, surrounding Frank and telling him their names. He couldn't possibly remember all of them, but he felt a great surge of pride and happiness as he looked at the eager faces of this raggle-taggle band. They were all hamsters who wanted to be free.

But another group hung back on the edge of the great machine. After several moments Frank went up to them.

'What do you want to do?' he asked.

These hamsters looked very timid, and several shrank back as Frank approached. They shuffled and jostled one another as he spoke to them, and at first no one answered his question, but then a small ginger-and-white hamster with no whiskers and broken teeth spoke. 'I – that is – we –' he began nervously, 'we think – we'd like to go home – if that's all right with you – that is?'

'*Home?*' said Rodney. 'Where's that then?' And there was a chorus of comments from the hamsters who wanted to go with Frank.

'Back to *humans*?'

'To a *cage*?'

'Mad, if you ask me!'

But Frank raised his paw again. 'I said that you are all free to choose,' he said. 'You must follow your instincts. If you want to go home, then go. No one will stop you.'

Immensely relieved, the small group scuttled away, over the edge of the big machine, to the substation floor. Once again Frank waited until they had gone, then he turned to the others. There were maybe thirty or forty hamsters waiting to follow him. Frank felt a prickle of excitement.

'Now I'm going to take you to your new lives,' he said, and for a moment he felt so overcome with emotion that he couldn't think what to say next. The hamsters all looked at him with simple, unquestioning faith. 'Things will be different there. There will be no one to tell you what to do. You will have to make your own decisions – live your own lives.'

He stopped again. How could he possibly describe to them what it would be like? They would have to live it to find out. It wasn't the time for big speeches. They should just set off.

'Follow me,' he said at last. 'I want some of the big ones to bring up the rear. Help any hamster that needs help.' And with that he set off, climbing down the ledges of the great, buzzing machine towards the entrance to the pipe. He didn't look back. He knew they were all following.

All the way back, as he led the hamsters through the pipeline and out into The Wild, Frank felt a fierce, solemn joy. This was what he had wanted all along. This was what all his visions of Narkiz had led him to, not to the Old Narkiz where wild hamsters had lived and

bred for generations, but to a new place where they could begin again. And for the first time he felt that it wasn't a disappointment that the past had gone, because this might, somehow, be even better. It was a powerful, heady feeling and it sustained him all the way back to the Great Chamber. As the concentrated scent of hamsters, fieldmice, voles and shrews replaced the jumble of smells in The Wild, he paused.

Two fieldmice appeared in the tunnel. 'Who's there?' said the first fieldmouse. He looked curious but unafraid.

'Tell George that Frank is here,' Frank said. 'And say

that more hamsters have come.'

The bright eyes of the fieldmouse blinked as he took in the queue of hamsters behind Frank, but he turned without saying anything and disappeared.

The second fieldmouse came forward. 'How many of you are there?' he asked. 'Coo,' he added, peering over Frank's shoulder at what seemed like hundreds of pairs of hamster eyes gazing back at him. 'You've brought a small army, mate. *How* many did you say?'

'I don't know,' said Frank.

He suddenly felt very tired, but happy. He could hear whispering among the hamsters behind him, but he didn't feel like talking. He sat back on his haunches and waited. Very soon he detected George's scent.

'Frank? Frank!' said George, nosing his way into the tunnel. 'Oh, you made it! I'm so glad!'

He came forward and Frank, without speaking, fell on his neck and hugged him. In that one embrace all their differences, their doubts and worries, disappeared. George pulled away and looked at Frank with shining eyes. Then his gaze travelled over the ragged crowd pressing behind him in the tunnel.

'You've brought reinforcements,' he said. 'Come in, come in!'

He stood to one side as the hamsters limped past, some of them helping others, and one or two on makeshift crutches. If he felt dismay at the sight of so many wounded, damaged hamsters, he was too polite to say so.

'Well – hmm,' he said as the last one hobbled past. 'Gosh.'

Frank pressed his shoulder with a paw. 'Can you cope?' he said.

'Oh, definitely,' said George, nodding vigorously. 'You leave it to me.'

Eventually the long queue creaked to a halt inside the Great Chamber. An awed murmur ran through the newcomers. It was already bigger than before and there were even more shrews, voles and fieldmice rescued by George and Capper. One hamster was helping a group of shrews to sort out some bedding for themselves, but, as all of Frank's hamsters piled in, she turned. It was Elsie.

'Frank!' she cried and ran towards him. They hugged, and Elsie kept saying, 'I'm so glad, I'm so glad,' over and over while Frank patted her shoulder.

Some of the new arrivals huddled together, gazing at this strange place that contained not only hamsters but all kinds of rodents. Frank could tell that it wasn't what they had expected, and they didn't know what to make of it. Now, at last, it was time to speak. Frank pulled himself away from Elsie and made his way to a large, smooth pebble and stood on it. All the hamsters and other rodents gathered round. As Frank gazed around he was struck both by the similarity to the Old Narkiz, with its great hall and pillars and the burrows leading off, and the difference. The old Narkiz had been inhabited by one kind of creature, the Syrian hamster, all golden brown and a similar size, but here there was a great assortment of rodents, and even the hamsters were all so different from one another. But they were

191

all waiting for Frank to speak.

'Friends and fellow rodents,' he began, looking round at them all, and for a moment he felt again that he didn't know what to say. But then he felt a deep sensation, like a powerful energy in the pit of his stomach, and all at once the words came. 'This is the dawn of a new era in your lives, and in the history of your races. Never before have rodents lived and worked together, but now, in this new territory, as long as you work together, you will thrive. This territory will belong to you and your families for generations to come. Together you can find food, ward off predators and live, free from human rule. In this Great Chamber you will make decisions about your lives and you will make them together, as equals. You are the Pathfinders for a new generation, for on this venture the future depends. We cannot return now to the old ways. Let no one try to divide you or rule. This is the New Narkiz!'

As Frank spoke, he felt the strangest, eerie sensation that he was speaking with the Black Hamster, or that the Black Hamster was speaking with and through Frank. The words came easily, because he followed what was being spoken in his mind, and he felt a powerful energy surge, almost as though the Black Hamster was actually inside him. The assembled rodents must have felt something of this, because as he spoke no one could take their eyes off him, and an absolute silence prevailed. The silence continued for a moment after he had finished speaking, then it was broken by an ear-splitting cheer that reverberated round the Great Chamber and turned itself into a great chant.

'Frank! Frank! Frank and the New Narkiz!'

And as the chanting continued Frank was lifted into the air and carried round the room. It was exhilarating, a moment of triumph, yet even in the midst of it all Frank couldn't feel totally carried away. An hour ago he had been passed over the heads of hamsters in the substation for an entirely different reason, but now he was the hero. It was a strange feeling.

After the excitement died down, the hamsters were shown round their new territory and some of them set to work right away to dig their own burrows. Elsie stayed with Frank, and George and Daisy came up to them.

'Well, Frank,' said George. 'We did it!'

Frank shook his head. '*You* did it.'

'I'd never have done it without you,' George said, and there followed the kind of conversation in which everyone tries to give everyone else the credit.

Finally Daisy said, 'Give over, will you? We all did it. That's the beauty of this place,' and she smiled at little Elsie, who was showing two of the more handsome hamsters around.

'You're right, my dear, as usual,' George said. 'I can't wait for you to find out what it's actually like to live here,' he said to Frank. Frank glanced quickly at Elsie, then away. The feeling had been growing in him that he couldn't stay, that, despite everything, this wasn't the place for him. He didn't know how to say it, but he would have to tell George. He cleared his throat.

'I – ahem – don't think I will be staying.'

George and Daisy stared at him in consternation. 'What?'

'I'm going back to the houses.'

George looked as though someone had just pushed him over.

'*Back to the houses?*' he exclaimed. 'Well – blow – me – down.'

Daisy put her arms round him for support.

'Is it – is it because – don't you *like* this place?' George said.

'It's not that,' said Frank. 'It's a wonderful place – you know that. Oh, I know,' he said as George started to interrupt, 'that I was a bit funny about it at first – that was me being stupid. Just because I hadn't built it, or because it wasn't the Old Narkiz. It's not that now, really it isn't.'

'Then what is it?' said George.

Frank sighed, then gestured towards all the other animals.

'You saw how they were with me,' he said, 'when I made my speech. They want me to be their leader – and that's the way it'll always be. It's almost as if they want something to worship, and I'll do. Then I can be blamed when things go wrong. No, wait,' he said as George started to interrupt him again. 'I'm putting this wrong. But as long as I'm around, these hamsters won't get on with running the place the way it needs to be run: by rodents who are free, and equal. Besides – you need someone on the outside.'

George looked bewildered. 'Why?'

'Well, someone has to tell other hamsters about this place,' Frank said. 'Mabel and Maurice and the pet shop hamsters – they aren't likely to stumble across it by accident – they have to be told. And if there's any more trouble, like the gangs and the fireworks, I can come and warn you. No,' Frank said, 'someone's got to stay in the human world.'

George stared at Frank, but he could see that he had made up his mind . . . and also that he was right, George had to admit that. It was useful, essential even, to have someone stay in the human world and act as a scout. But that Frank should be the one to do it, when all along he had tried so hard to escape, that was the surprise. George shook his head. 'Well, I don't know,' he said. Then he glanced up at Elsie. 'What about you?' he asked.

All the time Frank had been speaking, Elsie had not taken her eyes off him. Now she clasped her paws together, took a deep breath, and said, 'I think I'm going to go back with Frank.'

'Oh, *Elsie*,' George sighed.

'Let her make her own mind up, George,' Daisy said softly.

'I'm too used to living in a cage,' Elsie said apologetically. 'I've been treated very well there, and I'm very fond of my Owner. I'll come and visit, of course – see all my nephews and my niece.' She smiled at Daisy. 'It will make me feel better just knowing that you're all here. But if you don't mind, I think I'll be happiest going back, and knowing that I can visit any time I want. You don't mind too much, do you?'

George looked as though he did mind, very much, but Daisy said gently, 'Hamsters have to be here because they want to be here, Georgie – it won't work otherwise,' and he nodded and managed a smile.

'But you'll stay and eat with us,' he said, and Frank and Elsie said of course they would, and they helped to gather and prepare a splendid feast for all the new hamsters, and Elsie sat at Frank's right side. George looked at her once or twice as if he thought there might be more to her choice than met the eye, but Daisy kept nudging him and drawing his attention elsewhere: to the young shrews turning somersaults and to an older hamster dancing with a vole. And gradually he cheered up, so that when the time came for Elsie and Frank to leave, he was able to hug them both, beaming.

'Come back soon,' he said, and they both promised they would.

Then there was a flurry of paw-shaking and hugging and promises to meet again and placating some of the hamsters who had really thought that Frank would stay and govern them and tell them what to do.

Capper came forward and shook Frank's paw. 'I'd never have thought you'd go back there,' he said, and he seemed quite choked up. 'But I daresay you know what's best.'

'I don't know that I do,' said Frank, and he stopped, feeling choked up himself.

Capper nodded and stepped back as all the other rodents pressed forward to watch as Frank and Elsie disappeared into the tunnel.

'Take care of yourselves,' he whispered, hardly loud enough to be heard, but he *thought* he saw Frank turn round and wink at him. And then they were gone.

13 Home Again

Mrs Timms wandered round the charred ruins of her house. Most of the furniture had been taken away, and there were whitish squares on the wall where the pictures used to be. She had come back to leave cat food in the backyard in case any of her kitties had returned; but, looking round at the blackened, broken remains of everything she had once owned, her eyes filled with tears. She looked a sad figure in her faded blue dressing gown, with a big plaster on her nose. No one could understand how she came to have a bite-mark on her nose, but Jean had rubbed some ointment into it and given her a plaster.

'There you are, dear,' she had said. 'It'll soon mend, good as new.'

Arthur and Jean had been very kind, but she couldn't stay there forever. And her home wouldn't mend, good as new. The insurance money would come through eventually, and she could replace everything, but it wouldn't be the same. The woman from the council had said she could move into temporary accommodation while everything was sorted out.

Mrs Timms didn't really want to go into temporary accommodation, but she didn't want to impose any further on Arthur and Jean. It might take months for everything to be sorted out.

She wandered into the backyard with two saucers of cat food. 'Stinker? Tiddles?' she called softly, but no cats came yowling over the backyard wall. They had all been frightened off by the fire. Sadly Mrs Timms went back into the house. It all smelled of smoke, and charred wood. The birdcage had collapsed against the wall, and of course it was empty.

'Bobby?' she said, and her lip quivered. Then she picked up a length of wood that had once been a picture frame and poked behind the ruined cabinet. She felt it press into something that cracked, and there was a little tinkle of glass. Reaching down, Mrs Timms withdrew a photograph, still in its frame, though the glass had shattered. There, in the brownish tones of old photos, was the face of the young soldier she had married. It was a sensitive face, the thin lips in almost a straight line, but the eyes were kind. Mrs Timms clutched it to her dressing gown, in spite of the broken glass.

'Oh, Cyril,' she breathed, and tears dripped from the plaster on her nose. Then she caught sight of something else behind the cabinet and, reaching down, she pulled it out. It was her old cassette player, the kind that worked off batteries, and it still had a tape in it! Mrs Timms switched it on.

Immediately the small, charred room was filled with haunting music from gypsy violins. Mrs Timms took a

deep, wobbly breath. Then, still holding the picture of
Cyril to her breast, she began to dance.

Just at that moment, an elderly gentleman with silvery
hair and a walking stick was tapping his way along
Bright Street. It was Mr Marusiak. He had listened to
the complaints of all the different households in Bright
Street and he had just been to see Cheryl and Eric, to
warn them that they mustn't annoy their neighbours.

'WHAT ABOUT THEM ANNOYING US?' Eric
had boomed. 'OH, NEVER MIND, WE'VE HAD
ENOUGH. WE'RE OFF.' And he'd given in his notice
there and then.

Rather relieved that he hadn't had to tell them to
go, Mr Marusiak turned away. He called in at Lucy's
house to tell Angie the good news. It was Angie who
had called him in the first place, and she was delighted.
'I hope you'll be a bit careful next time,' she said.
'That's two problem tenants we've had.'

'It is the agency,' said Mr Marusiak, but he said he
had taken it out of the agency's hands now and would
be choosing the new tenant himself. Then he said
goodbye and returned to his car. But as he passed Mrs
Timms's house he was arrested by the sound of the
gypsy violins. He stood with his hand clasped to his
heart, as though something had just pierced it. Then,
because the door stood ajar, he tapped on it and, when
no one answered, he pushed it open and went inside.

There was Mrs Timms, swaying and bobbing and
pirouetting round the room in her faded dressing
gown, still clutching the picture of Cyril. Her eyes

were closed and she didn't see Mr Marusiak, but he stared at her as though he couldn't believe his eyes.

'Excuse me?' he said, in a voice barely above a whisper, then a little louder. 'Excuse me?'

Mrs Timms's eyes flew open and she gave a little squeak of alarm. Her hand clutched at her robe. Then she peered at Mr Marusiak 'What – ?' she said.

They stared at one another without speaking. Then Mr Marusiak said, 'The music – from the old country?'

Mrs Timms blinked in amazement, then she said slowly, 'The Duna Bar.'

'The gypsy violins – and the little lanterns – I was there – I was there after the war!'

Mrs Timms looked as though this was too much to take in. Mr Marusiak stepped forward as though he would embrace her, but she was still holding the photograph of Cyril. He took it from her gently. 'Your husband?' he said.

Mrs Timms bowed her head. 'I'm alone now,' she said.

'Me also,' said Mr Marusiak, and he was silent for a long moment, gazing at the young face in the photograph, but all he said was, 'He looks as though he was a good man.'

'The best,' said Mrs Timms, and her eyes filled with tears.

There was so much they had to say to each other, about the Duna Bar, and the war, and about what had happened after. Mr Marusiak had worked as a waiter in the Duna Bar, then more wars had come, and revolution, and he had fought one enemy after another, but finally he had to leave the country he loved, just as Mrs Timms had left to marry Cyril. And now, here they both were, in Bright Street! It was astonishing that they hadn't met before, but Mr Marusiak didn't live there himself, of course. He had bought the first house five years ago through an agency, and they rented it out for him, so that he was hardly ever there. And Mrs Timms had lived in that same street for nineteen years, but she didn't mix with the neighbours and only went out to buy gin and cat food. But now, all these years and countries later, they had met up like this!

There was so much to say that they couldn't begin. Then Mr Marusiak said, 'Do you remember the cats, outside the Duna Bar? I used to feed them.'

'Me also!' cried Mrs Timms and she told him that she still fed the cats, but then she looked around anxiously. 'They've gone, my kitties,' she said, 'since the fire,' and she told Mr Marusiak what had happened. 'I call to them but they don't come,' she said. 'It is because the house has gone and they have no home.' Her eyes filled with tears.

'But – I have a house,' Mr Marusiak said. 'Right here in Bright Street. And soon it will be empty again. You are welcome to stay there, until the work is done.'

Mrs Timms's face lit up so that she looked once more like the young, pretty girl she used to be. 'You mean it?' she breathed.

'I would be honoured,' said Mr Marusiak, and he bowed.

Mrs Timms blushed. 'Mr Marusiak –' she murmured.

Mr Marusiak put the photograph down. 'Pierre,' he said, 'And I can call you – ?'

'Natasha,' said Mrs Timms, but it was as if she was suddenly shy. She wouldn't look at him but kept plucking at the edge of her shabby dressing gown.

'Natasha,' said Mr Marusiak tenderly. 'Shall we dance?' And he started the cassette again and held out an arm. Hesitantly at first, Mrs Timms stepped after him. She took one step, then another, and soon they were waltzing round the ruined room.

They made an odd couple, Mr Marusiak a little stiff, but stately, with his silver hair and black suit, and Mrs Timms in her faded dressing gown and floppy slippers, with the plaster on her nose; but he beamed down at her and she beamed up at him, and it seemed as though all the years, and all the different countries they had travelled through, had come together in the little shabby room.

Meanwhile Frank and Elsie had arrived back at Elsie's house. No one was in, but her cage still stood near the window of the front room. It looked a little forlorn, but Lucy had left the lid off in case Elsie should return, and every day she filled her bowl with fresh food. Elsie got in straight away and gave a little hop and a skip because she was so pleased to be back; then she set about rearranging her bedding and almost forgot about Frank. He smiled to see how happy she was to be home. 'Well, I'll be off then,' he said.

Elsie stopped immediately, midway through stuffing some of her bedding into her pouch.

'Oh, Frank,' she said, 'thank you so much – for saving me from the fire, and leading me through The Wild – and everything – I can never thank you enough.'

'Don't mention it,' said Frank modestly. 'I'd better be on my way. I'll stop off and tell Maurice and Mabel about the New Narkız. Not that they'll be interested,' he added. 'But still, they ought to know.'

'I suppose so,' said Elsie. She looked at him anxiously. 'Oh, Frank – you will be careful, won't you, in Maurice's house – there is the cat.' She could hardly say the word 'cat' without a shudder.

Frank was about to say that, after everything he'd been through recently, a cat seemed like a small problem; but he reminded himself that it was never a good idea to be overconfident in the face of any kind of danger, and he said, 'I will be careful, I promise. And you, too – take care of yourself. If you have any problems or worries – well – you know where I am.'

'Yes,' said Elsie gratefully. 'And we will go and visit George again, won't we?'

'Of course we will,' said Frank. 'Very soon. Well – I'd better leave you to sort yourself out before Lucy comes back.'

'Yes,' said Elsie again and she looked at him wistfully. There were so many things she wanted to say, but she couldn't find the words. She reached up and poked her nose through the tiny bars at the top of her cage. Frank hesitated, then leaned forward and touched his nose to hers. 'Goodbye, Frank dear,' she whispered.

'Goodbye,' Frank said, and then he was gone, over the edge of the coffee table and across the carpet to the

skirting board and through a familiar chink to the Spaces Between.

Elsie watched him go, one paw still raised in farewell. Then she sighed and looked round her cage again. There was a lot to do to get it just the way she liked it, but she couldn't resist running round her wheel a little first, just to remind herself what it felt like, then she familiarized herself with all the old smells in each chamber and thought to herself how much nicer a hamster cage was than a birdcage. She burrowed in and out of the soft wood-shavings in her sawdust chamber and reorganized her bed, but though she was tired by now and ready to curl up, she didn't want to miss the look on Lucy's face when she returned. So she had a drink and filled her pouches with food and waited, gazing out of the window, for Lucy to come home.

Next door, in Jackie's house, Frank had a hard time waking Maurice up. He tapped on the bars, then climbed on top of the cage and rattled them. Fortunately, Sergeant was asleep upstairs on Jackie's bed, and the children were out with Jackie at a community fireworks display for Bonfire Night. When Maurice still didn't wake up, Frank opened the cage door and went right up to Maurice's bed and called his name.

Eventually Maurice poked his nose out of his bedding. 'Oh, it's you, is it,' he said irritably. 'Can't you see I'm trying to sleep?'

This wasn't a very promising start, but Frank still felt that he had to explain to him about the opportunity to live in The Wild. He cut his story short and simply said that George had set up a new colony for hamsters and for any other rodent who wished to live there, free from human rule.

Maurice listened with a bad grace, then when Frank had finished he shook his ears free of bedding and said merely, 'Is that it? Can I go back to sleep now?'

Frank gave up. 'Just thought you'd like to know,' he said, and he set off without wasting further time, through the Spaces Between to Mabel's house, passing beneath Mrs Timms's with its unpleasant odours of charred wood and cat wee, and Arthur and Jean's house, until he came to number 11, which smelled of perfume and discontent. He travelled across the thick pink carpet with bits of fluff and food clinging to the strands (Mrs Wheeler hoovered even less often than Guy) and climbed the rough material of the armchair until he was facing Mabel's cage, where Mabel was sleeping the sleep of the overfed.

Mabel woke up at once as Frank approached, and she stared at him with her disconcerting gaze. 'Well?' was all she said.

Frank took a deep breath. He didn't relish this part, but he was determined to let every hamster know that they didn't have to live in a cage if they didn't want to, that there was a choice.

Unlike Maurice, Mabel listened patiently and made Frank go over bits of his story again, about the fire, and the humming hamsters, and the New Narkiz. She groomed herself as he told his tale, but she was listening, though when he finished she said merely, 'Is that all?'

Frank was annoyed. 'How much more do you want?' he said.

'Oh – I don't know,' said Mabel silkily. 'What about your friend – the Black Hamster? You haven't said much about him.'

Frank looked at her suspiciously. He had left the Black Hamster out of his story because he knew what Mabel thought of him and he didn't want to get into an argument.

'What about him?' he said.

'Dear me,' said Mabel. 'Don't tell me you haven't heard from him recently? He hasn't disappeared, has he, in this imaginary country? Just like an imaginary friend?'

'He's not an imaginary friend,' Frank began hotly, before reminding himself not to get involved in any argument. He didn't care whether she believed him or not.

'Of course not,' said Mabel soothingly. 'Well, that was a very nice story – quite the best I've heard for a long time. But it's made me quite sleepy. If you don't mind, I think I'll go to bed. If you know any more stories, you could tell them to me while I settle in.'

Frank stared at her and opened his mouth to tell her what she could do, then he started to grin. For, standing just behind her cage, and a little larger than it, was the Black Hamster of Narkiz.

'I always like the one about the tooth fairy,' Mabel continued, patting her mouth as she yawned. 'Or the Easter Bunny – that's my favourite. But you choose,' she said, turning around. Then for quite a long moment she said nothing at all.

'Hello, Mabel,' said the Black Hamster, with a ferocious grin.

Mabel tried to speak, but all her words died away into a rattle at the back of her throat. She tottered backwards, then her eyes rolled back in her head and she fell to the floor of her cage in a dead faint.

'Mabel!' Frank cried.

'Leave her,' said the Black Hamster, and with a single

bound he joined Frank on the back of the chair. 'She will wake in a moment, and will tell herself that it was all a dream.'

Frank stared at the Black Hamster. 'How can you stand it?' he said.

'I speak to the hamsters who will listen,' said the Black Hamster. 'And I speak through them to the others, if they will let me.' He smiled at Frank and Frank smiled back at him, feeling suddenly very happy. Then the Black Hamster said, 'You have done well, my son,' and they embraced. Frank felt thrilled and proud, and sure somehow that everything would work out. He didn't even mind any more that he wasn't going to live in the New Narkiz, but in a cage for the time being, because he knew he still had his part to play.

When the Black Hamster released him and said, 'Shall we go?' Frank ran with him down the chair back and across the carpet and through the chink in the skirting board that led to the Spaces Between. It was here, long ago it seemed, that Frank had first heard the Call of the Black Hamster, and so much had happened since that time! Now, though they didn't speak, Frank felt that they understood one another very well, and there was no need to ask questions, because soon they would meet again.

The Black Hamster paused as Frank was about to enter his new domain.

'There is much to do,' he said. 'I will come back.'

For the first time Frank didn't need this reassurance. He was completely and happily sure that he would see the Black Hamster again. He said nothing, but smiled.

The Black Hamster bowed deeply to Frank, and suddenly, briefly, there were stars, and hundreds of thousands of other hamsters, stretching away in time and space as far as the eye could see, all bowing to Frank. Overcome, Frank bowed in return and, as he looked up, the Black Hamster touched his nose briefly to Frank's and once again Frank felt the surge of power.

'Go well, my son,' the Black Hamster said, and he was gone. Frank looked around and he was in the dusty, musty space that was beneath the gas fire in Guy's front room. He sighed deeply, but it was a sigh of great happiness, and he began to scramble upwards through the space in the slates.

Guy was on his way home from a friend's house. He had passed Mr Wiggs's pet shop on the way and hadn't been able to resist looking in. Frank had never been missing for so long before, and the house felt empty without him. If he had really gone this time, Guy thought, then maybe, just maybe, he should think about getting another hamster. Not that any hamster could replace Frank, of course; but still, there was the empty cage, and Guy missed having someone to sing to. He scanned the big tank that stood as usual in the window of Mr Wiggs's shop.

There was a cluster of tiny hamsters, all sleeping together in a huddle. As Guy watched, one of them detached himself from the group and began to scramble over his brothers and sisters towards the window. There, just as Frank had done, he pressed his paws

against the glass and stared at Guy. Guy felt a terrific pang. He raised a finger to the pane and the little hamster looked as though he was trying to bite it through the glass. He was just the same colouring as Frank, Guy noticed: golden brown and white. He could call him Jeffrey.

But Guy couldn't bring himself to replace Frank just yet. He gazed regretfully at the little hamster. 'Not yet, little fellah,' he said, and turned reluctantly away. He walked home with a heavy feeling in his heart. And he let himself in, thinking all the time about the sad song he would compose in Frank's memory.

Without noticing Frank, he went straight to his guitar and sat down with it, beginning to strum. Frank went to the front of his cage and rattled the bars, then rattled them again.

'Not now, Frank,' Guy said. 'I'm composing. I'm making up a song about you. I –' He stopped.

'*Frank!*' he breathed and he fell to his knees. 'Oh, Frank, Frank!'

Frank didn't want a big emotional scene so he did a little caper. Guy picked him up immediately, stood up and did a little dance that almost exactly imitated Frank's. Frank hopped about and shook one leg, and Guy did the same.

'Where have you been?' Guy said. 'I've been so worried about you – oh, but never mind,' he said, dashing his tears away with the back of one hand. 'It doesn't matter – you're back now – you're back!'

'Yes,' Frank thought, looking up at Guy with an only slightly rueful grin. 'I'm back!'